THE FEAR OF GOD

By the same author

The Limbo Connection
The Solstice Man

THE FEAR OF GOD

DERRY QUINN

BARRIE & JENKINS
COMMUNICA - EUROPA

©Uniworld S.A. 1978
First published in 1978 *by*
Barrie & Jenkins Ltd
24 *Highbury Crescent, London* N5 1RX

ISBN 0 214 20530 4

Printed by Anchor Press and
bound by Willm. Brendon Ltd.,
both at Tiptree, Essex

For
BRIAN

CONTENTS

At 9 a.m. on Tuesday, 11 September Gerald McDermot stepped into a black Mercedes 250 outside his home in Netherhall Gardens, Hampstead, North London. As he did so a bomb exploded under the car, almost completely demolishing it and killing him instantly. McDermot, managing director of the Acropolis Publishing Company, was fifty-three years of age.

Part One
THE HOUND OF HEAVEN

Wednesday was the day Fred returned to the flat after one of his long, inexplicable absences. It was also the day the girl threw herself off the roof.

The two incidents were quite unconnected. Fred's comings and goings had always had a random quality as independent of human affairs as the passage of some distant star. Neither a harbinger of doom nor a companion to dire events, he simply came and went as it pleased him or as he was compelled by whatever outlandish laws determined his behaviour.

His place was the scullery: a narrow room some thirty feet square with an ancient sink under the window and a galvanized iron water tank up on the far wall. Here and only here, for his own cosmically obscure reasons, did he make his presence felt.

Paul Marriott shivered slightly as he turned to the paint-peeling wall behind the scullery door. Fixed to the wall was a thermometer and beside this a large sheet of cardboard upon which Jill had kept a record of Fred's arrivals and departures. The last entry was nearly three years old. For a long time he stood staring at the rows of dates; they were written in pencil, Biro, a bright orange felt pen – whatever Jill had been using at the time for making out the laundry lists. The record had been precisely kept over a period of more than five years. Together they had tried to plot Fred's visits against the seasons, the phases of the moon, family events, the prevalence of thunderstorms and changes in atmospheric pressure. Yet no discernible pattern had ever emerged. The only constant factor they had been able to establish was that Fred never turned up during the period of the

Earls Court Motor Show.

Paul looked closely at the thermometer. The mercury registered forty degrees. The temperature in the rest of the flat, at the height of this September heatwave, must already have been nearly seventy. The air in the scullery was curiously still; not the slightest draught came through the open window. Here, within the confined space of the back kitchen, the laws of nature had been temporarily suspended.

He crossed and took a packet of cornflakes from a shopping basket on the floor. 'Hello, Fred,' he said quietly. 'It's been quite a while.'

From the mews behind the block he heard a slow plodding of hoofbeats and the rattle of a cart. 'Aiee-o-ayo! Aiee-o-ayo!' The sad-sounding cry of a hawker drifted up through the silence. He glanced out. On the back of the cart was an old gas cooker, part of a bedstead and a few lengths of piping. Any old iron. The man was leading his horse, the heads of both bent under the breathless heat, between the tall housebacks of the empty mews. The relic of a long passed and forgotten London, the hawker came this way every three months or so collecting scrap.

Going to the kitchen door now, he looked round briefly. 'So long, Fred me old chum,' he said. 'Have a nice day.'

'Aiee-o ayo! Aiee-o ayo!'

As he came into the kitchen, the warm air wrapped itself around him. It was like stepping out of a tomb. He made a pot of tea, filled a bowl of cornflakes and sat down to his solitary breakfast. The flat was silent except for the low persistent rumble of traffic in Earls Court Road.

Talking to Fred had always been a custom in the household. He and Jill had adopted the practice mainly for the sake of the children. As soon as Naomi and Jonathan had been old enough to understand, they had introduced them to the idea of Fred's presence, had discussed his comings and goings quite openly, as if it were the most natural thing in the world that the flat should be haunted. They had always prided themselves on the enlightened and sophisticated way in which they had brought up their children. Like sex, nakedness and one's bodily functions, Fred's presence in the scullery was nothing to be furtive about; it was just another fact of life, neither more important nor more mysterious than any other.

'Do you think Freezy would like some breakfast?' He could suddenly hear Jonathan's voice as if the boy were standing behind him in the kitchen.

'Freezy can't eat, silly. He's got no tummy.' Naomi's laugh. So like Jill's.

'Poor old Freezy!'

'Aiee-o ayo! Aiee-o ayo!' The hawker's voice came, scarcely audible, from the top of the mews.

Paul finished his cornflakes and tea. He had hardly been out of the flat for a whole week and he felt edgy. Big as the place was, with its four bedrooms and two huge reception rooms, he had had the sense of being hemmed in. The week had been spent hammering out a long article for *Manhattan* magazine. It was a good piece. The Americans would like it. And for the kind of money they paid, well worth the solitude. A week out of his annual holiday. In fact, the job had taken him less time than he had expected. He didn't have to report back to his newspaper until Monday. The prospect of five days' hanging about the flat didn't appeal to him; particularly with London largely emptied of friends for the summer season. He would look in at the news room this afternoon, he decided; talk to David Plummer, try to get a story off the ground.

Going to the sink, he washed up his cornflake bowl and cup. He shook the tea-leaves from the pot into the refuse bin under the sink. The bin was overflowing. He would have to carry it all the way down the bloody stairs and round the corner to the back area. A job he hated and one which Mrs Yabsley, who came in to clean three times a week, resolutely refused to perform. There had been a time when he had been able to put the bin in the service hoist beside the sink; the porter, calling a respectful 'Good morning, sir', had hauled it down and emptied it. But the new landlords had got rid of the porter at the same time that they had put the passenger lift out of commission and sacked the woman who came in to clean the main stairway. They wanted to turn the block into profitable bedsitting rooms, which meant making life as inconvenient as possible for the tenants while offering them inducements to get out. Five thousand pounds was the current offer. Three of the tenants had already taken their money and gone, leaving Paul on the top floor and old Mr and Mrs Kolokowski on the ground floor.

He wondered sometimes why he didn't move. Though the controlled rent was ridiculously low, he could have afforded to pay more for a modern bachelor flat with proper services. Earls Court Mansions belonged to another age. Built at the turn of the century to house solidly respectable Edwardian families with several children and a servant, it had long outlived its purpose. He had moved in sixteen years ago when he had first married Jill. Naomi and Jonathan had been born here, had all but grown up here. Not that he was staying out of sentiment, he told himself. Perhaps if Mr Dowding, the landlords' managing agent, had been less high-handed, he might have been more inclined to listen to reason. He didn't like being pushed. So the more Dowding harassed him, the longer he would stay. Flat E, The Mansions, was his home and his castle. An empty castle, it was true; a haunted one even. But Jack Dowding with his waspish voice and hectoring manner would have to take the roof off before he budged. He stood a moment staring out of the window, realising that the explanation was not entirely satisfactory. The new firm had taken over less than a year ago. It was three years since Jill had gone off with the children.

Turning sharply from the window, he picked up the cornflake packet and put it on the sideboard. As he did so, he became aware of the still, unnatural coldness in the scullery. No one had ever seen Fred except Mrs Cole, a garrulous and rather simple-minded woman who had come to look after the children once when Jill had been away. Mrs Cole had described him as a young man in Edwardian dress: 'Handsome as you please with curly black hair and a chalk-white face–such a passionate look on it, with his blazing dark eyes, it would take your breath away. Hanging about after one of the serving maids, you can bet your life.' For a moment Paul stood frowning across the empty room. A horn blared somewhere in the distance; a window slammed in the mews. He left the kitchen.

A long passage decorated with ivy wallpaper led past the master bedroom and bathroom, past another bedroom and another bathroom, to the front of the flat. He paused for a few seconds at the open doorway of the first of the two big rooms that looked down on Earls Court Road. About thirty feet by twenty, the same size as the living room next door, it had once been the children's playroom. Faded grey curtains with faded yellow flowers at the half-barred windows; stains of spilled poster paint on the worn grey carpet; marks on the walls where they had Sellotaped their pictures. Mrs Yabsley had cleaned out the room a few days before and had left one of the cupboards half-open. He had always meant to take the old toys to a children's hospital: a lidless box of dominoes; a plastic bag filled with multi-coloured balls of Plasticine; a Boeing Flying Fortress painted in fairground colours, a stick of purple bombs under one wing; a dolls' house that looked as if it were waiting for a demolition gang; a red plastic gramophone that once played 'Jimmy Crackcorn' and 'Carbon the Copycat'. They would be listening to pop music now, Paul thought. Naomi had been fifteen last month.

He went on down a longer passage, his footfalls silent on the dark green carpet; his study to the left, the living room to the right. He remembered Naomi's early passionate letters to him after she had arrived in Canada. 'Daddy, Daddy, Daddy' they had begun. Two letters a week at the beginning, they had soon dwindled to one a month. Now he only heard from the kids at Christmastime: how they were doing at school, how Naomi had won an essay prize, how they would soon go skiing with Mummy and Josh. Josh Pennellier, the bearded Canadian advertising agent whom he had never for a moment suspected of having designs on Jill. Strange, since it had seemed so obvious in retrospect. But then he had been too busy, too absorbed in himself, to notice. A grey winter afternoon: he had just turned the lights on in the living room and had been crossing to pull the curtains. 'I want a divorce, Paul,' Jill had said. He had stopped and looked at her sitting with her back to him before the lighted fire. He had known at once that it was Josh, the truth hitting him with a terrible suddenness; a jarring moment of illumination. Like a man who had been slapped across the face and woken rudely from a long dream, he had stood staring at her back. After thirteen years of marriage he had somehow come to feel that he and Jill had lived together all their lives; that he would always return from his newspaper assignments – from Amsterdam, from Paris, from Hong Kong – to find her here, the calm centre of his domestic life, in the great rambling flat with the two children. It had never occurred to him for a single moment that she might consider any other man more attractive than he, that it would ever cross her mind to be unfaithful to him. Wrapped up in himself and his ambitions – and, it was true, enjoying a few casual affairs in the course of his work – he hadn't bothered to read the signs, all that Josh's appearance in their lives six months ago had portended. 'Josh has asked me to go to Canada with him.

6

I want to take the children,' she had said very softly, her voice hardly audible above the noise of the traffic in the street below. Without a word he had gone on across the room and drawn the curtains. Like a thunderbolt it had hit him. The most shattering blow he had ever sustained in his life.

Turning now at the end of the passage, he went along the hall and opened the front door. On the mat outside was a pile of newspapers. Reading all the London dailies had long been part of his morning routine. Gathering up the papers, he made his way to the study.

He had left the window open all night and the room was cool. Facing an area at the back of the block, the sun seldom reached it in any case. The walls were pale coffee-coloured, the carpet off-white and the curtains maize and blue. It was a businesslike room with three steel filing cabinets and a stationery cupboard on one side, a grey leather sofa and armchair on the other. Black-painted bookshelves covered the wall behind the desk; above the sofa was a reproduction of Picasso's *Guernica*. The desk faced the window.

He sat down and pushed aside the notes he had been using for the *Manhattan* story. Among them were several photographs of himself, one of which he had posted to New York with the article. He had chosen the picture with care, a portrait taken a year ago in which he appeared smiling and relaxed, his greying hair razor-cut and styled the morning he had visited the photographer. He thought the shot made him look a little younger than his forty-two years without seeming ironed out or lacking in character. It was one he meant to go on using for some time to come. The lighting, he thought, was particularly effective: it gave his darkly handsome face a leanness it did not quite possess and revealed, without in any way accentuating, the long thin scar that ran from the corner of his right eye to the corner of his mouth.

Noting that the time was exactly ten o'clock, he started

to scan the papers. The lead stories on all the front pages were about the car bomb incident in Hampstead the previous morning, the murder of the publisher Gerald McDermot. They told him little more than he had already heard on the BBC news the night before. One paper went so far as to say that the bomb had probably been of the pressure type, fitted to the suspension of the car and designed to explode under the weight of the driver. Another commented on the fact that up to now no terrorist organisation had claimed responsibility for the killing. There was no background of any kind on McDermot, what he published or why he should have been a target for assassination. The stories had been written, Paul could see clearly, under the shadow of a fistful of D notices. D for defence: official warnings that the publication of certain material would not be in the national interest. There would be little point in his, or anyone else's in Fleet Street, attempting to pursue the matter. Whatever sinister facts lay behind the murder, the public would never hear about them. Uncovering ugly truths was his business and he knew how many and how formidable were the obstacles that government agencies could put in the way of a hard-digging journalist. No, he could forget about Gerald McDermot.

He continued to read. The room was quiet. Scarcely a breath of air came through the open window. The heatwave had lasted nearly a month now, the sun blazing down out of a hazy colourless sky, the streets heavy with the smell of petrol fumes. Reaching for a pair of scissors, he cut a two-column story from one of the papers. A group of Scottish nationalists had tried to sabotage a pipeline from one of the North Sea oilfields. It was a subject he could discuss with David Plummer, his News Editor. A well-researched story on the security measures protecting the oilfields would be worth keeping on file. A couple of weeks in Scotland; an excuse to get out of London. Certainly there was little enough to keep him here.

Sitting back a moment, he found himself thinking about Penny Armstrong. His most recent affair. It had lasted two months, which was about average for him. Penny had taken off a couple of weeks ago, down the long, unswept flights of stairs from the flat, to sit on a crowded beach in Spain and think about their relationship. He had been supposed to think about it, too; but somehow he hadn't got around to the task. Penny was always talking about relationships, as if they were things you put together like Meccano. He only hoped she wouldn't come back from her holiday and decide they should go on relating. If she did, he would be better off in the North Sea.

He felt he had had the best of Penny. It was time for a change. Putting the scissors on the desk, he slipped the cutting into a folder at his elbow. It was a little disturbing to think that he had lost count of all the girls who had come and gone during the past two years. They had all been young; he preferred them under twenty-five – the birds he picked up at parties, in pubs and in people's offices. The knowledge that he was irresistible to women gave him a curious sense of security. He depended upon it as another man might depend upon alcohol or tobacco. His sex life had just that addictive and compulsive quality; and it afforded him no lasting satisfactions. That this had become an unalterable feature of his emotional make-up he had long ago admitted. Since Jill and the children had left him, the possibility of his entering into any permanent relationship had simply ceased to be part of his scheme of things. Whether it was an act of revenge, or the expression of some obscure and half-apprehended despair, or whether he had merely reverted to type, he had never been able – nor did he really wish – to determine. But like the drinker, one amorous adventure only seemed to create the need for another. It was the ritual, he decided, the so often repeated ritual that mattered. You caught a girl's attention; you chatted her up; you

9

took her to bed. You kept her around for a while, until again you felt compelled to repeat the pattern of encounter, pursuit and conquest. For better or worse, it filled the empty places in his life as nothing else could.

He stirred uneasily in his chair. Penny, Gillian, Marie-Thérèse, the little mathematics teacher from the Lycée in South Kensington. He could recall the more recent ones. The names and faces of the others seemed to fuse together in his mind until they became one nameless face, one anonymous naked body in bed beside him. He stared out of the window. The clatter of a dustbin lid came from the hollow silence of the yard below; the sound of limping footsteps moving away. Mr Kolokowski from the ground floor. In all the years Paul had lived at The Mansions he hadn't exchanged more than a dozen words with him. Kolokowski's wife was a tall, big-boned woman like an eagle. They had three mortice locks on the front door of their flat which they turned laboriously every time they went out and turned again behind them when they went in. The area gate creaked and slammed on its spring. The lame footsteps faded along the pavement. A milk float went whirring by. From somewhere, a child's shout and the thud of a football. Paul turned back to the newspaper.

It was then he heard the shriek; a half-shriek cut off as if in astonishment, coming from close by and just above him. Looking up, he saw something hurtle past the window. He remembered registering surprise at the speed at which it was falling; a brief, blurred vision, a flash of something black and white. The impact came before he expected it, seeming to follow almost immediately upon the cry: something soft and quite light slamming on to the concrete. He didn't move at once. It had all happened so incredibly quickly. He found himself trying to rationalise what he had seen and heard, his mind struggling to reject the idea that there was a body lying in the yard outside. Perhaps he had only imagined it. He would look out and there would be no body. It was nearly half a minute before he got to his feet, crossed the room and put his head out of the window.

Fifty feet below him, a girl was lying in the area. She was lying on her back at the top of a short flight of steps leading from the porter's flat. She was wearing a rather grubby white T-shirt and dark blue jeans; sandals on her feet, a silver bracelet glinting on one slender wrist. She had light reddish hair cut very short and a small pointed face. Her eyes were wide open. The only sound to be heard was the rhythmic thudding of the football on the pavement down the street.

The telephone was on his desk. Reaching for the receiver, he dialled 999 and said, 'Ambulance.' He was connected immediately. The man at the switchboard questioned him in slow, measured tones that suggested a rocklike imperturbability: his name, his address, his telephone number, the exact location of the back area. He had no sooner finished than the operator cut in and said, 'You have to inform the police in cases like this. I'll put you through.' Another granite voice came over the line, this time from the Information Room, and Paul went through the whole routine again. Finally he put down the phone and left the room.

A moment later he was hurrying down the staircase, past the empty flats and the stranded lift, to the hallway. Pulling open the front door, he stepped outside, the heat and noise of the street hitting him all at once.

A group of youngsters carrying bright orange rucksacks looked strangely at him as he pushed his way past them and headed down the pavement. Taking the first turning into Bramham Gardens, he walked quickly round to the mews. The gate squeaked as he opened it and he entered the yard.

He went to within a few feet of the girl and stopped. She was quite evidently dead, her face ash-coloured, her mouth half-open. She had green eyes. He thought how thin she looked, dirty and uncared for. He could see little

11

blue veins showing under the skin at her temples; a scattering of freckles on her small delicately shaped nose. She was very pretty, with her high cheekbones and pointed elf-like face. He thought she couldn't have been more than twenty years of age. Turning his head, he looked upwards. The back rooms of Earls Court Mansions had been built out from the main part of the block so that their southern windows faced the blank rear wall of the neighbouring apartments in Bramham Gardens. A fire-walk, protected by a low parapet, ran along the edge of the roof from one block to the other. From where he stood, he could see the top of an attic door opening on to the fire-walk just above his study.

The air was hot and still. Flies buzzed around the dustbins behind him. A bicycle bell sounded in the mews. He walked back to the gate and stood waiting. The windows on the other side of the mews belonged to flatlets and bed-sits usually empty in the daytime. Strange that someone could jump from a roof-top in the middle of a crowded city and not be seen. He wondered who the girl was and why she had done such a thing. A piece of newspaper, caught in an updraught of air, rose and went scraping across the concrete. Somewhere along the mews a radio was playing.

Ten minutes later a police car appeared, coming slowly round the corner. Paul stepped out on to the pavement and signalled to it. The car stopped; a sergeant in uniform and a constable got out. 'This way,' Paul said, leading them to the area.

He stood watching as the two policemen went and looked down at the body. After a moment they came back to him and the sergeant said, 'It was you who reported this, sir?'

'Yes. My name's Paul Marriott. I live on the top floor there. Flat E.'

'And you saw her fall, sir?'

'From my window.' Paul pointed upwards. 'She must

12

have jumped from the parapet directly above.'

The sergeant looked up at the roof and the open window, then turned to Paul. He had very small dark eyes and a grey leathery face set in a permanent expression of weary scepticism. 'Did anyone else see it happen?'

'Not as far as I know. There's only one other tenant living in the block. The place has been taken over by property developers.'

'Do you know who she is? Did you ever see her before?' The sergeant hadn't taken his eyes off him.

Paul shook his head and looked towards the roof again. 'We get squatters up in the attic there. You can see where the fire escape door is. Seems to me that's where she came from.'

'Squatters, sir?'

'Youngsters coming in off the street. I hear them going up and down the stairs sometimes. There's no porter in the block now, the front door's left open day and night.'

The sergeant looked away from him at last. 'We'll come up and take a statement from you as soon as the ambulance has been.'

'Very well.' Paul turned. 'They're taking their time, aren't they?'

'Coming from Chelsea, it would be the traffic, sir.'

'I dare say.' Paul opened the gate and went out into the mews.

Entering the hallway of the block, he closed the door against the turmoil of the street. Inside, the place was as silent as always; the lift hanging darkly between the first and second floors like a dead animal in a cage. The faint sound of a vacuum cleaner came from the Kolokowskis' flat. On the wall beside him was a varnished notice board displaying the names of the tenants; next to each name was a wooden slide which you could move back or forth to show whether you were *In* or *Out*. Flat E. Mr and Mrs Paul Marriott. Flat D. Mr and Mrs A. R. L. Stapleton-Bretherton. Flat C. Miss K. A. Simpson. Flat B. Cmdr

J. H. Whitney-Green. Flat A. Mr and Mrs V. Kolokowski. The gold-leaf of the lettering had peeled in places where somebody had scratched a swastika across the board.

He started up the stairway. He had always prided himself in being able to climb quickly up the four flights without losing breath. He practised karate twice a week at a club in Holland Park and did physical exercises every morning. His footsteps sounded loud on the gritty stairs as he ascended. Months ago someone with an aerosol tin had sprayed a serpentine pattern of black paint across the wall on the second floor. Several carrier bags filled with refuse lay dumped on the third landing where the aerosol artist had written *Pigs* on the wall. He was breathing quite evenly as he reached his flat, but he didn't stop. Instead he went on up the two remaining half-flights to the door that led to the attic. The door was ajar. Beside it was a little red-painted box marked *Fire* which had once contained the key. The glass front of the box had long ago been smashed and the key taken from its hook. He pushed the door and went in.

It was stiflingly hot in the low, dim space under the roof. The light was on, a single bulb hanging from a long flex among the rafters. Strewn around was the debris left by earlier squatters: empty boxes of Colonel Sanders's Kentucky Fried Chicken, milk bottles, beer cans, the remains of a sliced loaf mouldering in a packet, a yellow plastic hat and numerous carrier bags in various stages of disintegration. Hanging over the nearest beam was a pair of laddered tights; a picture of Al Stewart, fixed with Sellotape to the rafter above, flapped gently in the draught from the open door leading to the roof.

Ducking under the beams, Paul went to the door. Here he paused and looked down. Lying just inside the threshold was a dark green sleeping bag and a small fibre suitcase. On top of the case was a mug with 'Ovaltine' written across it. A tartan duffle bag, a pair of men's shoes protruding from the top, stood against the wall near by.

14

He went on through the doorway. A platform protected by a low railing led to the fire-walk and the parapet. He reached the parapet in time to see the ambulance enter the mews. Two men got out and took a stretcher from the back. While the constable held the gate open, they carried the stretcher into the area and put it down by the girl's body. One of the men said something to the sergeant, then with a swift, practised movement they lifted the body on to the stretcher. The ambulance driver arranged the girl's arms, crossing them in front of her. The other unfolded a geranium-coloured blanket and together they laid it over the body. The red of the blanket looked disturbingly brilliant under the white opalescent light of the sky. Two remote, foreshortened figures, they carried the stretcher back across the area to where the constable was still standing with his hand on the gate. Paul left the parapet and went back into the attic.

It would have taken the girl only seconds to walk from where the sleeping bag lay to the edge of the roof. He wondered if she had acted on the spur of the moment or if the deed had been something long premeditated. Getting down on one knee, he took the Ovaltine mug from the top of the suitcase. He was about to lay it aside when he put it to his nose and sniffed; the mug smelled strongly of aniseed. He put it on the floor and opened the lid of the case. Inside was a sponge bag, a pair of black panties and a worn paperback edition of *The Cloud of Unknowing*. He closed the suitcase and looked briefly at the sleeping bag. The grimy pillow still bore the faint indentation of the girl's head. He leaned forward and reached out his hand. Protruding from beneath the pillow was the corner of a notebook. He pulled it out and got to his feet. The cover was creased and stained, the pages dog-eared. No name or address outside or inside; the pages filled with what appeared to be verses.

Turning to the light of the doorway, he looked more closely. Verses they were, written in a large, sprawling and

15

curiously uncontrolled hand, hurriedly and without correction. He stood a moment, leafing through the book, glancing at a phrase here and there. Then gradually he found himself reading with more attention. The verses, if indeed they were her own, had a sombre, haunted quality that stirred his imagination. Whoever the girl had been before she pitched herself into oblivion, she had surely been something rather special; no ordinary sensation-seeking youngster living from hand to mouth through a London summer, but a highly sensitive and gifted creature with a remarkable originality of mind.

For some minutes he stood leaning against the door-frame, reading slowly. When he heard the footsteps of the policemen coming up the stairs he straightened and closed the book. It would have been an easy thing to toss it on to the sleeping bag. But he hesitated; he wanted to read more, and in any event the notebook contained nothing that would help the police to identify the dead girl. The two men were coming through the doorway on the other side of the attic now. On a sudden impulse he pushed the book into his trouser pocket, then went forward to meet them.

The sergeant and the constable bent double as they came under the beams. The sergeant gave Paul a mildly inquiring look but said nothing. He walked forward, paused to look at the sleeping bag, then made his way out on to the roof. The constable remained, standing beside the girl's possessions as if he were guarding them. After a moment the sergeant returned and came to where the bedding and the suitcase lay. 'These would be her things?' he said to Paul.

Paul shrugged. 'I don't know. Presumably.'

'You've no idea how long she'd been sleeping here?'

'None. As I said, I hear people on the stairs from time to time. I don't pay too much attention.'

The sergeant eyed him for a moment, then nodded. Kneeling down, he put the mug aside and flipped back the lid of the suitcase. He glanced at the paperback, shook the panties and emptied out the sponge bag: comb, toothpaste, toothbrush, a little box of eye make-up and a rusty pair of nail scissors. Turning, he pulled the pillow aside, then lifted the sleeping bag and peered underneath. Evidently he was looking for drugs. Getting to his feet at last, he brushed his trouser legs and went to examine the contents of the duffle bag. Apart from the shoes, his search revealed a razor kit, a pair of jeans and a crumpled pullover.

Taking a notebook from his pocket, he moved nearer to the door. 'If you'd like to tell me exactly what you saw, sir,' he said to Paul.

Paul told him what he had seen. It was little more than he had reported over the telephone.

The sergeant wrote it all down and put the book away. 'Thank you, sir. That'll be all, I think. If we need you again we'll let you know.'

Paul gave the two men a nod and made his way across the attic.

Back in his study, he took the notebook from his pocket and sat down. He was still reading the verses when he heard the policemen descending the stairway outside. Very probably they would never identify the girl. There had been nothing to give them the slightest lead, not so much as a bus ticket.

Down in the mews, the doors of the squad car slammed; the engine started and the car pulled away, heading along Bramham Gardens. The radio was still blasting pop music through an open window somewhere near by.

It was nearly half an hour before he put the book aside and rose to his feet. The time was nearly eleven o'clock. If he were going to get through the daily press before lunch, he had better hurry.

Resolutely he continued his study of the papers. He had been 'off the diary' in the news room for more than a year now; he did no routine reporting but was free to follow his own lines of inquiry. The trouble was, he hadn't come up with a workable idea in the past two months. He had pursued half a dozen stories in that time, but for one reason or another they had all come to dead ends. Either key informants had decided not to talk or libel writs had been threatened; or, as in the case of a series he had tried to write about a mental hospital in the Home Counties, vested interests had been too determined to keep the lid down. None of this was unusual; it was part of the job. All the same he was worried.

His career as an investigative reporter had begun just before Jill left him. Covering a bullion robbery at London Airport, he had persuaded his News Editor to let him do a series of pieces on the then severely plagued crime-prevention system at Heathrow. During his years as a crime reporter he had developed a remarkable talent for investigation, a flair for unearthing the truth that would have been the envy of any policeman. After weeks of painstaking inquiry around the airport he had been able to go the police with evidence – and enjoy the exclusive rights on the story – concerning collusion between a gang of thieves and one of the country's leading security guard organizations. His 'Thiefrow' series had been a sensational success; it had won him acclaim as a journalist and, for a time at any rate, the gratitude and trust of his Editor.

What he was looking for now was something to top his last feature on the Chinese Triad gangs and the Soho heroin trade. The job during which he had lived for weeks among the drug addicts around Piccadilly. The stories he had written about these people, particularly the young-sters, he considered to have been the best work he had ever done. He had got his scar on that assignment. Cornered in a Soho alley by three men from the Triad 14K gang, he had been obliged to fight for his life. Only his skill at karate had saved him. As a result, one of the gangsters had nearly died of a fractured skull when Paul had knocked him to the pavement. A few nights later an

18

officer of the Vine Street Drug Squad had been severely beaten up in reprisal. The police had taken a grimly serious view of the affair and he had been warned off the territory.

The fact was, his honeymoon with the police had ended with the 'Thiefrow' articles. Shortly afterwards he had dug up the notorious Robbery Squad corruption scandal which had brought him into head-on collision with more than one influential figure at the Yard. The Robbery Squad, part of the C8 Flying Squad, had always been regarded as the crack force in the Metropolitan area. Operating out of Rotherhithe and Leman Street in East London, their job was to break up the big-time gangs while leaving the detailed investigation to local officers. Their work was such that it could only be carried out by men of absolute integrity. Yet Paul's inquiries, conducted among criminals, middlemen and ex-prisoners in the East End, had revealed an elaborate network of corruption involving at least nine members of the seventy-five-man squad. Four-figure sums had changed hands in some deals; evidence had been falsified on charges going before the courts so that juries could not return proper verdicts; at the same time money had been demanded to prevent fabricated charges being laid against men with criminal records – a technique known as 'fitting up'. When Paul's copy and all the statements and tape recordings had been handed over to the A10 internal investigation branch at the Yard, he had been interviewed by the Squad's Chief Superintendent, a man called Meedon. Meedon had tried to persuade Paul and his paper to withhold publication of the material on the grounds that it would have a bad effect on the morale of the force. Nonetheless the paper had gone ahead and printed the stories. Meedon had had several close friends in the Robbery Squad, two of whom had resigned during the inquiry that followed. The Chief Superintendent had recently been promoted Commander, Serious Crimes, at the Yard; a fact that wasn't going to be particularly helpful to Paul in his career.

When he had finished reading the papers, he spent half an hour going through his files. Here were subjects he had begun to research and which for one reason or another he had set aside. He was scraping the bottom of the barrel; but there might just be something worth discussing with Plummer. He had done a lot of work on the militant left wing organisations in Britain, the communist 'peace' fronts and the anarchist and Trotskyist secret cells; the South American hit man 'Carlos' and the Popular Front for the Liberation of Palestine's underground network in London and Paris. There was the Lincoln Towers story about a high-rise block in central London, containing flats for several hundred families, that had remained mysteriously empty for the past eighteen months. Then a bulky folder on international arms trading. All good stuff; but short on news value. He closed the cabinet and went into the living room. He hated being without a story. It was like being without your right arm.

The sun was blazing through the front windows and he lowered the venetian blinds. The pale green walls gave an impression of coolness to the room. There was a faint smell of furniture polish that would linger until Mrs Yabsley's next visit. The room pleased him. It had taken over a year to put together. Weekend after weekend he and Jill had visited auctions and country sales looking for exactly the pieces they wanted. There wasn't a chair, a table, an ornament he didn't remember buying with her. Going to a corner cupboard by the door, he poured himself a small vodka and carried the glass to the kitchen. From the fridge he took a lemon, ice and a bottle of tonic. He drank little but was always very precise about the way he prepared his drinks. He cut a slice of lemon and poured the tonic. The radio was still blaring through the open window down the mews. A number that seemed to be on the air all the time just then:

20

Love, love,
I want someone to love.
Someone to cry with,
Live till I die with,
Someone to love.
Someone to sing with,
Have me a fling with,
Someone to love.
Yes! Yes! I want someone to love . . .

He finished his vodka, put the glass on the draining board by the sink and went into the bathroom. At the mirror, he ran a comb carefully through his hair, noting that he was due for a visit to the barber. Adjusting the roll-neck of his white Terylene jersey, he took a grey linen jacket from the back of a chair and put it on. For several seconds he stood studying the effect. He had gained a little weight. Too much sitting around. He must take more exercise; have no more than a salad lunch on his way to the office.

The street was hotter than it had been when he had come down to look at the dead girl. He paused on the front step, the bell pushes and the entryphone hanging half-wrenched from the wall beside him. He would walk to South Kensington, he decided.

By the time he had covered the fifty yards to Oakeshotts, he was already sweating. On the other side of the street a small group of people stood staring curiously at the ruined frontage of the Taj Mahal food store. The place had gone up in flames during the early hours of Wednesday morning. It was rumoured that someone had put a fire-bomb through the letter box. A smell of roasted curry powder mingled with the stench of exhaust fumes. Turning the corner, he was relieved to find himself in the comparative quiet of Old Brompton Road.

The news room was on the fourth floor of the paper's steel

21

and glass building. It was two hundred and fifty feet long by forty feet wide. Here all the reporters and most of the special correspondents had their desks. There were few people around at this hour, their figures small and oddly stylised-looking in the vast perspective of the room.

David Plummer's desk, chaotically untidy as always, was nearest the door; at his elbow the battered portable radio through which he listened to the news broadcasts; in front of him an array of telephones. He was sitting sideways, his legs crossed, eating an apple. 'Hello, Paul,' he said. 'Didn't expect you till Monday.'

'I thought I'd drop by, see what was going on in the world.'

'Nothing you haven't read in the newspapers.'

'Are you sure?' Paul gave him a smile, pulled up a chair and sat down.

Plummer dropped the apple-core into a wastebasket. He was a big, bald man with a face like one of the more disreputable Roman emperors, an explosion of black brows above a pair of dark, perfectly round eyes. 'No filthy corruption, no dirty cover-ups, no vile conspiracies. No one being bribed, blackmailed, persecuted or intimidated. We've had a very clean week, funnily enough.' He sat a moment staring at a packet of chocolate biscuits in front of him. 'You got any bright ideas?'

'What about the Lincoln Towers story?' Paul said. 'Those flats standing empty off Russell Square because Metropolitan Securities want to make a tax loss.'

Plummer shook his head. 'Too dangerous. Metropolitan would sue us if we so much as published a photograph of that bloody block. They've as good as said so. I admit it's worth a write-up, but remember caution is still very much the policy upstairs. There'd be no point in suggesting it even.'

Paul nodded. The paper had lost heavily in two libel cases during the past year; losses they could ill-afford. A suit filed by Metropolitan Securities wouldn't be for

peanuts either. So he told Plummer about his other ideas:
the North Sea oilfields, the terrorist organisations and the
arms trade.

Plummer responded by pursing his lips in an expression
of doubt and disapproval. 'They're all a bit long-term,
aren't they? Sleepers. And any one of them would keep
you pinned down for weeks.' He paused to watch,
Caligula-like, as a pretty secretary went by. Plummer
neither smoked nor drank and was unhappily married.
From time to time he would make a furtive pass at one
of the girls in the news room; but none of these ever
seemed to come to anything. 'Merlin was asking about you
at yesterday's news conference,' he told Paul, taking a
chocolate biscuit from the packet. 'Wanted to know what
you were coming up with. I'm afraid he's in one of his
restive moods.'

Paul felt a twinge of uneasiness. Merlin was the Editor.
Howel Thomas, to give him his real name. He had once
been dubbed 'the Welsh Wizard', principally for having
rescued two ailing tabloids during the 1960s. Who had
first called him Merlin, no one knew; but somehow the
name had stuck. He had become Editor of the paper just
over a year ago and was busy steering it, if not to pros-
perity, then at least off the shoals of bankruptcy. A great
many heads had fallen in the process. Certainly he wasn't
a man to tolerate passengers on his staff.

'I told him you'd be interested in doing a piece on
rabies,' Plummer said.

'Rabies?'

'A lot of people have been prosecuted during the
summer for smuggling pets into the country, some of them
sent to prison. It's a talking point just now. Make a good
spread for one of the weekend editions.' Plummer spoke
with the air of a man who was as anxious to convince
himself as his listener. 'We all know rabies is a deadly
menace and has to be kept out. But you could try to
dig up something controversial. One or two smugglers

have been caught because neighbours informed on them. Would you report your best friend for spiriting a hamster out of Dieppe? Are we overreacting to the danger? Is the law being too severe or not severe enough? What about modern vaccination techniques? Have a think about it. Also talk to Eddie Campbell. He covered some of the court cases earlier on. Might give you a lead. He should be around somewhere.'

Paul got to his feet. 'Very well,' he said without much enthusiasm. 'I'll go see.'

He left Plummer reaching for another chocolate biscuit and made his way down the room. Stopping at Eddie Campbell's desk, he looked about him. There was no sign of the reporter. The rabies story would be a chore. There was nothing new in it. Something Plummer had produced off the top of his head to placate Merlin. Paul would write the piece and everybody would say he was slipping. He could only hope to God that something better turned up.

> Thus my prayer,
> Shaped like a tear,
> Short as a flower on fire,
> Compounds all saying's need
> On this occasion.

He had said nothing to Plummer about the girl throwing herself off the roof; the girl and her book of verses. They weren't news. But the memory of the incident wouldn't leave him. He kept seeing her falling past his window; her green eyes staring at him from the area well; her verses singing in his head.

'Helen . . .' He looked round as a tall, dark-haired girl went by; the secretary he shared with Campbell. 'Have you seen Eddie?' he asked.

'He slipped out a while ago, said something about Gray's Inn.' Helen's face always softened slightly when

24

she spoke to Paul. 'Can I get you a cup of coffee?'

'Yes. Thanks.' He went to his own desk and sat down. There were a few letters for him. Two were from cranks: a man offering to sell him information about unspecified 'rotten practices in a certain borough council office'; another from someone who believed he was being persecuted by the police and signed 'Mr Jack Addis, The Man Who Knew Too Much'. He threw them both in the wastebasket. Helen brought the coffee and he drank it slowly. If Eddie had gone to Gray's Inn to talk to one of his legal cronies, he might be away for hours. He finished the coffee and sat looking out of the window, wondering how he would pass the time till Monday. Finally he got up and left the news room.

At about six o'clock he went to the living-room cupboard and poured himself a Scotch, one of the two he usually permitted himself when he was on his own in the evening. He took the glass to the kitchen and got ice from the fridge. Drink in hand, he crossed and looked into the scullery. The place was warm, a gentle breeze blowing in through the open window. Fred had gone.

He was carrying his drink back along the passage when he heard the sound of footsteps, the slap-slap of sandals going up the stairway past the flat. Moving to the hall, he set down his glass and opened the front door.

The footsteps halted immediately. He could see nothing, for the intruder was on the other side of the lift cage, on the second half-flight leading to the attic. The silence continued as Paul climbed the first half-flight round the well of the stairs.

A young man was standing just above him, his back to the attic door. He might have been nineteen or twenty, tall and very thin. He had long fair hair and hadn't shaved in several days, a silvery down-like growth of beard on his chin. His face was very pale, ascetic-looking and disarmingly innocent. He was wearing a green shirt

25

buttoned at the wrists and a pair of jeans.

'You looking for somebody?' Paul asked.

The boy didn't answer, regarding him distrustfully through a pair of almost colourless eyes.

'It's all right,' Paul said. 'I'm not the landlord. I live in the flat down there.'

The boy hesitated. Then he jerked his head towards the attic door, 'I came to collect my stuff,' he said very softly.

'A tartan duffle bag?'

The other nodded, still watching Paul warily.

'You were with the girl, then? The red-headed girl?'

The young man gave him a long, searching look. 'Yes.'

'I'm afraid there's been a bit of trouble,' Paul said. 'She — had an accident. The police were here this morning.'

The boy said nothing. The mention of the police seemed to have alarmed him. For a moment Paul thought he was going to take off down the stairs. But he didn't move.

'Look, why don't you come down and have a drink? We can talk about it. I'll tell you what little I know.' Paul started down the stairway. For a moment there were no following footsteps. Then he heard the flap-flap of the sandals behind him.

The boy came into the flat. Paul closed the door, collected his drink and led him to the living room. 'Sit down,' he said, pointing to an armchair by the fireplace. 'What would you like? A vodka? Whisky?'

The other sat down rather uneasily and looked round. 'I couldn't have a glass of wine, could I?'

'Sherry's the best I can do,' Paul told him.

'Yes. I'll have a sherry. Thank you.'

Paul poured the drink, brought it to him and went to a chair on the opposite side of the hearth. 'How well did you know the girl?' he asked.

'Rosamond Clay?' The boy took a sip of sherry and looked down at his glass, turning it between his long fingers; his hands were sweaty and streaked with dirt and there was black under his fingernails. 'Not very well,' he said in the same hushed voice he had used on the stairs, 'I mean only a few days really.' He looked up. 'What happened?'

'She went out on the roof,' Paul said. 'And fell. I saw it happen. I called the police. They came around. I couldn't tell them very much.'

The boy sat for a few seconds without moving. 'She threw herself off.'

'Yes.' Paul waited. The young man didn't seem anxious to volunteer any more information. 'How did you meet her?' Paul asked.

'Oh . . . Round here. I ran into her late one night. She was wandering the streets, carrying that sleeping bag of hers. I'd been using the attic for some time, so I took her up there.'

Paul had been watching the boy closely. There was little doubt in his mind that he was a junkie; probably on heroin. The pallid, sweaty skin; the contracted pupils of his rather fixedly staring eyes. These things were not certain indications in themselves. The real giveaway was the rolled-down sleeves. 'Was Rosamond Clay on drugs?' he asked.

The boy drank some sherry, then shook his head. 'No. Not the hard stuff anyway.' A faint expression of puzzlement passed across his face. 'She was living on a mixture of purple hearts and Pernod.' He twisted the glass in his hand, looked up and said quickly, 'She was really screwed-up, freaked out, a little crazy.'

Paul got to his feet and went to the window. 'We haven't introduced ourselves. My name's Paul Marriott.'

'John Aubrey.'

Paul walked back down the room. 'You've no idea where she came from?'

'No.' Aubrey paused. 'I believe her parents lived at a place called Tarrybridge. She used to talk about a disco pub in the World's End, the Lord Kitchener. I think she had friends there.' He turned to Paul and gave him a faintly guarded and inquiring look. 'Why are you so interested?'

Paul shrugged. 'Human curiosity. I also happen to be a newspaperman.' He came over to the hearth. 'Is there anything else you can tell me?'

'A bit, yes.' Aubrey finished his drink and sat holding the glass in both hands. He seemed to make a visible effort. 'What's it worth to you?' he asked suddenly in a voice that didn't sound quite like his own.

'Nothing, really,' Paul replied. 'I'm just a little intrigued.' He looked at Aubrey. He felt suddenly sorry for the boy. He put his hand in his pocket. 'But if you could use fifteen quid. I haven't much more on me.'

The other nodded, looking down at the carpet. Stepping forward, Paul proffered the money. Half the price of a fix in Romilly Street, he thought. Aubrey took it with a swift, rather furtive movement and put it in his pocket.

'Well?'

'I only know there was this other girl – Gail Canning . . .' Aubrey was frowning at the floor again. 'Rosamond had got into one of her really bad states. There were times when she'd lie for hours, just crying. She said she had to go and see Gail. It was the first time she'd ever mentioned her. She kept saying, "I've got to see Gail, I've got to see Gail" – kind of hysterical, you know. I didn't want to let her go off on her own. I mean, anything could have happened to her. So I went along.' The boy looked up slowly. 'Gail Canning was keeping her supplied with purple hearts. When we got there, they had a big row. I think because Gail wouldn't give her enough hearts.'

'How many was she taking?'

'Ten or twelve a day.'

'So what happened?'

'They were rowing. I didn't hear everything they said, just a bit now and then. They were in the bedroom and the record player was on. Rosamond started shouting and screaming, saying she was going to kill herself. Then I heard Gail laughing at her.' Aubrey put his glass down on a table beside him. 'There was something about a doctor in Wimpole Street, but I couldn't make much out of it. I think Gail Canning said, "You be a good girl and go back to the doctor, I'll give you all the purples you want. No doctor, no purples." It sounded like that anyway. When Rosamond came out of the room she was crying. She ran straight for the front door and I followed her.'

'Didn't she say anything to you afterwards? Didn't she explain?'

'No. I think she was too scared. In any case, nothing she ever said made a lot of sense. She used to – sort of ramble. Most of the time you couldn't tell what she was talking about. And then she'd go for a day or more without saying anything at all. . . . I don't think she knew where she was half the time.' Aubrey got to his feet and stood a moment rubbing the palms of his hands against his jeans. 'I felt sorry for her. She was a nice girl. She was really nice. You could tell.'

'What do you think was wrong with her?' Paul asked.

'I don't know. She'd blown her mind. She was bombed. Perhaps she'd had a bad trip, it's hard to say. I never met anyone like that before.' The boy stood perfectly still for a moment, his curiously ravaged face sombre and thought-ful. He said very quietly, 'I used to think sometimes she'd been frightened out of her wits. I mean, quite literally. She'd been frightened so badly, she didn't even know what had happened to her. She couldn't bring herself to contemplate it. I know it sounds strange, but that's how it struck me.' He paused briefly, then went on in the same hushed tone. 'She was living in terror of something or somebody. I'm not sure, but I think it had to do with that disco.'

'The Lord Kitchener?'

'Perhaps.' Aubrey frowned. 'She was always going on

about a disco. About "going down to the disco". Or sometimes she'd say "the Music Room" – "going down to the Music Room". I could never make anything of it. It was all muddled up with other things. All freaky, you know.'

The windows rattled as a lorry thundered past the block. Paul walked away and stood for a few seconds looking down at the rush-hour traffic, the crowds hurrying along the pavement, the sun blazing on the roofs of the cars. 'Where does Gail Canning live?' he asked.

'St George's Yard. Off Warwick Way. A flat with yellow window boxes.'

Paul returned to the fireplace and put down his drink. 'Rosamond Clay wrote verse. You know that?'

'Yes.' For some reason the wary look came back into Aubrey's face. 'You saw it, then? Her notebook.'

Paul nodded.

'She used to sit out on the roof and write. After she'd had a lot of Pernod. She said she could remember then. I thought her stuff was pretty good.'

'It's very good.'

'Did the police go off with her things?' Aubrey asked.

'Probably. I haven't looked.'

The young man gave a little nod. Then he said, 'Do you mind if I use your lavatory?'

'Sure. On your right at the bottom of the passage.'

Aubrey left the room. Paul made his way back to the window and stood staring down at the street again. He heard the lavatory flush, the door open and close. It seemed a long time before John Aubrey reappeared at the living room door. The young man stopped and looked briefly along the passage, an expression of mild astonishment on his face. 'Do you live here all by yourself?' he asked.

'Yes. Most of the time.'

'Christ.' The other man moved on towards the hall.

Paul followed him and opened the front door. Aubrey

stepped out on to the landing and said, 'I'll just go up and collect my bag.'

'Where are you going?'

'I've found a new pad. I'd come to tell Rosamond. A place in Shepherd's Bush. There are more people and it's not as hot as the attic.' He moved to the foot of the stairway, looked round and gave Paul a faint, boyish smile. 'Thank you for the sherry,' he said

Paul watched him go up the stairs, then he closed the door and made his way thoughtfully to the study. Here he spent a moment looking up a number in his address book. He lifted the telephone receiver and dialled.

The bell rang briefly at the other end and a voice said, 'Kensington Police Station.'

'My name is Paul Marriott. I live at Flat E, Earls Court Mansions.'

'Yes, sir?'

'I reported an accident this morning. A girl threw herself off the roof here.'

'Oh, yes?'

'I've just been talking to someone who was able to identify her. I thought you should know.'

'One moment, please.'

There was a long pause. Then the policeman came back on the line. 'It seems the young woman has already been identified, sir. She was carrying a driving licence. But you'd better give me some particulars.'

'The person I talked to is called John Aubrey. Aged about twenty. No fixed address.'

'Oh, I see, sir. . . . Well, thank you for telling us.'

'Not at all.' His duty done, Paul put down the telephone.

A few minutes later he left the flat and walked round to the mews. His car, a bright red Triumph Stag, was parked against the area wall.

He made slow progress through the heavy traffic along Old Brompton Road, through South Kensington to

Victoria. He hoped Gail Canning would be home. In any case it would have been useless to telephone her; almost certainly she would have refused to speak to him. He had long ago learned the value of personal confrontations. It was far more difficult for someone to slam a door in your face than it was for them to put down a receiver. And he was suddenly very anxious to talk to the Canning girl. The more he thought about what Aubrey had told him, the more bizarre the whole business seemed. Gail Canning had been bribing Rosamond Clay with purple hearts so as to persuade her to see a doctor – the one person who would have prescribed drugs to alleviate her condition. It was illogical to say the least. If Aubrey were right and Rosamond Clay had been frightened out of her mind, then what conceivable horror could she have witnessed? And in a discotheque of all places. Perhaps Gail Canning would be able to tell him. True, none of it might make news; it might not cause David Plummer to raise so much as an eyebrow. But the dead girl had been in his thoughts all day. Now his conversation with Aubrey had posed questions that clamoured for an answer. He wondered about Aubrey. Somehow he couldn't rid himself of the idea that the boy had told him less than he knew. There had been something furtive, something a little sly, about his manner. What, though, could he possibly have to hide? Frowning, Paul turned out of Harrington Road and followed the crawling traffic round Cromwell Place.

St George's Yard was a cobbled area of lock-up garages beyond a cream-painted arch. A man in shirt-sleeves and gumboots was hosing down an Austin Princess in one corner. The flats were above the garages, approached by a flight of concrete steps. He could see the yellow window boxes in front of a blue door to his right. Climbing the steps, he rang the bell. There was no reply. He rang again. All he could hear was the splashing of the hose. Turning, he went back down the steps and climbed into his car.

The rush hour was at its height as he inched his way along King's Road. There was an interminable wait at the pedestrian crossing by the Safeway supermarket, people ambling by, tired and listless from the heat. Pop music blared through the open doorway of a tatty clothes shop. The traffic moved at last, only to meet another snarl-up at Flood Street. There were a few drinkers standing on the pavement outside the Markham Arms; he noticed that the leaves of the trees in Markham Square were beginning to turn. Just short of the town hall he was held up again, this time by a group of punk rockers who stepped suddenly off the pavement in front of his car. There were four of them and they stood close together staring at him with blank, hostile expressions. The two men were wearing black shiny vinyl pants; one of them had an SS skull and crossbones cap on his head and a nail driven through his right ear lobe; the other wore a camouflage jacket with a parachute harness over his shoulders and a dog collar round his neck. Both girls had dyed their hair a sulphuric yellow; the first had heavy make-up only on her left eye, the other only on her right eye; one wore a bike lock round her neck and the other a lavatory chain. Somewhere behind, a car horn bleeped impatiently. The rockers showed no inclination to move. Paul sat back and waited. Finally the man in the SS cap leaned forward and very deliberately spat on the windscreen. Then beating his fist on the bonnet he shouted, 'Anarchy! Self-rule! Believe in yourself, you piss pot!' Seemingly satisfied, they turned and started walking away down the middle of the street.

Five minutes later Paul reached the World's End. Parking in a side road, he locked the car. He had never been inside the Lord Kitchener before, though he had noticed it often enough in passing.

The place was only a short walk away, a rather seedy-looking Victorian pub distinguished by its windows which had been painted jet black, each with a huge white eye in the centre. Replacing the conventional inn sign was a large notice above the door: 'Lord Kitchener's Disco' written over a Union Jack.

Coming in off the street, the bar seemed almost impenetrably dark. The music was folk rock, blasting tone-distorted through overloaded speakers, a mind-numbing acoustic guitar and the voice of Al Stewart. Paul knew the recording; it was a good one; he only wished that the owners of discotheques would pay more attention to their equipment. Crossing the floor, he knocked into one or two people before his eyes became accustomed to the gloom. There were few places to sit: low tables with uncomfortable-looking mushroom-shaped stools over to one side. Above the bar, black on white, was a pop-art representation of Kitchener's moustache. The inevitable 'Your Country Needs You' poster hung near by; steel helmets, gas masks and limp khaki uniforms draped here and there. Covering the whole of the end wall was a huge photo-mural of a First World War soldier: clutching a rifle, his eyes tortured and hollow with battle fatigue, he gazed in frozen anguish down the dark, noisy room. Paul reached the bar. There weren't more than half a dozen customers: the kind of teenagers you would see in the Chelsea Drugstore, the Trafalgar or the Bird's Nest. The barman turned to him and he asked for a lager. When the man brought it he said, 'I'm looking for a friend of mine, used to come here quite a bit. Girl called Rosamond Clay.' He had to raise his voice, half-shouting above the din of the music.

The barman shook his head. 'Sorry, I wouldn't know. I'm only temporary. Ask the guv'nor. He'll be down in a minute.'

Paul picked up his glass and turned his back to the counter. The music had changed to a piece of sleazy, twelve-bar blues; a ten-year-old Pink Floyd number. The door opened and a group of young people came in from the street. Crossing the room, they moved to the far end of the bar. Paul sipped his drink thoughtfully. He would give it a quarter of an hour, he decided, see if the landlord turned up. It was just possible the man might remember Rosamond Clay or be able to point out someone who had known her. Failing that, he would go back to St George's Yard later in the evening.

He had nearly finished his drink when the door opened again and the four punk rockers entered the pub. They came half-way across the floor and stopped, looking towards the bar. In the dim light they appeared even more grotesque than before. A spotlight on the ceiling threw deep shadows across the face of the youth in the Nazi cap; the girls' oddly painted faces showed deathly white in the gloom. They stood motionless, seeming a little lost and uncertain, like a group of clowns that had somehow wandered in on the wrong act. The boy in the SS cap was standing a few paces in front of the others. Raising his voice above the music, he suddenly shouted, 'I hate Pink Floyd!' A few people at the bar turned their heads, though without any great show of interest. Just then a man who looked as if he might have been the landlord appeared from a back room near the bar; he was about thirty and wore a brightly coloured sports shirt. When the two girls and the boy in the parachute harness saw him they turned and walked nonchalantly out of the pub. The youth in the skull and crossbones cap came on across the floor and stopped beside Paul. He watched the landlord go behind the counter, then, looking around, realised all at once that he was alone. He must have felt that some gesture was required of him and he seemed to ponder the question. Paul regarded him with interest. The most astonishing thing about him was his ordinariness: he had a loose mouth and a round, immature pudding face; his eyes, small and rather close-set, were without a glimmer of intelligence, expressing only a dull and half-perceived resentment of the world; his peaked cap was far too small for him, perched on top of a greasy mass of hair. He stood there, leaning his elbow on the bar, a pathetic caricature of evil. The landlord had come up and was looking across the counter at him with frank distaste. The youth turned his head and, without much conviction in his voice, shouted, 'Try subversion, man!' With that he marched away to the door.

The landlord gave a shrug and smiled at Paul. 'I know what I'd do if I was his father,' he said. 'The Sex Pistols – you heard any of it? I wouldn't play that stuff here, not for all the money in the world.'

A guitar solo was coming through the speakers so that it was just possible to converse without actually yelling. 'Most of the kids don't like it either,' he said.

'They're darned right. It'll die the death – you see. I wouldn't insult them with it.'

'Mostly regulars, are they?'

The landlord nodded.

'You wouldn't happen to know a girl called Rosamond Clay?' Paul asked. 'Red-head. Used to come here once.'

The bass guitar and drums were coming up behind the solo now. The landlord leaned a little way over the counter. 'Who?'

'Rosamond Clay!'

The man shook his head. 'Might know her if I saw her. It's faces here, not names. Know what I mean?' He moved on to where a couple of jean-suited young men were waiting for drinks.

Paul set down his empty glass and turned to see that someone was looking at him; someone he hadn't noticed before, an extraordinarily attractive young woman standing in the shadows at the far end of the bar. She was with the group that had come in during the Pink Floyd number. The people she was with were all in their teens, but he would have put her age at about twenty-seven. Her dark hair was cut very short; she was wearing hotpants and a T-shirt with 'Patrice Lumumba University Moscow' printed across the shapeliest pair of tits he had seen in a long time. She gave him a smile. He smiled back at her, wondering if perhaps the evening were going to take an unexpected turn. He had been on the point of leaving; the idea of a casual pick-up had been far from his thoughts. But he had come here to find out what he could about the disco, and here might be an opportunity. The music was still blasting away, seeming to make the very air vibrate with its noise. She had turned her attention back to her companions, two long-haired boys and a slim girl in a white kaftan.

He guessed she might be waiting for the end of the number. Sure enough, when it finished and the next one began with a mercifully muted piano solo, she left her friends and started in his direction. She had a very sexy way of walking, poised and unhurried. He noticed that her eyes were almost jet black and that she was wearing no make-up. She had that scrubbed, clean look, the fresh and uncomplicated kind of face that very sex-prone women sometimes possessed.

'Hello,' he said as she stopped in front of him.

'Hello.'

'Would you like a drink?'

'No, thanks.' She leaned her elbow on the bar. 'I heard you asking about Rosamond Clay just now.'

'Why, yes. Do you know her?'

'Very well.' She regarded him quizzically for a moment. 'I was interested. I wondered who you were.'

'A friend of hers, naturally.'

The girl's very dark eyes hadn't left his face. She shook her head almost imperceptibly. 'I know all Rosamond's friends.'

'Really? Are you sure?'

'Quite positive.'

'I mean, even her family's friends? People in Tarrybridge?'

'I don't think Rosamond had much to do with her parents' friends. Certainly not in Tarrybridge. If you'd said Maidstone, where they lived before, I might have believed you. Just.'

'All right,' Paul said. 'I don't know Rosamond Clay. But I do know she got herself into some kind of trouble. Serious trouble. Something rather complicated. I'm looking into the story for my newspaper.'

'You're a journalist?' The girl gave a little frown of puzzlement. 'Why would a newspaper be interested in Rosamond?'

'They might well not be,' Paul replied. 'But I have a nose for these things. I'm incurably inquisitive. A compulsive lifter of lids.'

'When your nose tells you there's something underneath?'

He nodded. 'Look, you knew her. Perhaps you can help me.'

'*Knew* her?'

The music had got suddenly loud again, a cascade of noise from an acoustic guitar filling the room. He bent close to her, catching the sharp animal scent of her skin. 'She's dead!'

The girl stood staring at him for a moment. 'We can't talk here,' she said quickly. 'There's a pub across the street.' She glanced down the bar at her companions. 'Give me a few minutes.'

The floor seemed to be jumping under the impact of the music. It was pure noise, the banging, screeching rhythm of guitars and drums. There had been a time when Paul had been able to sit for hours listening to this kind of thing. Now the din was like a physical assault on his nerves, pulsating inside his head and making thought impossible. He said to the girl, 'I'll wait for you there.'

She nodded and moved away.

It was with a sense of relief that he stepped out on to the hot pavement. The roar of the traffic sounded almost pleasant after the pandemonium of the disco. Crossing the street, he went into the pub. The doors were open against the heat; the place was almost empty, the landlord in shirtsleeves reading a newspaper at the bar. Paul ordered another lager, took it to one of the tables and sat down facing the doorway.

She came in five minutes later, walking towards him in her easy, graceful fashion. Heads turned as she crossed the floor. She had the kind of figure for which hotpants had been designed; the longest pair of legs he had ever seen.

He stood up as she approached. 'What can I get you?' he asked.

'I don't happen to drink. An orange juice would be fine.'

He went to the bar and got the orange juice. Putting it on the table, he sat down and said, 'I'm sorry I broke the news to you like that. It must have sounded very brutal. But discotheques don't lend hemselves to civilised conversation.'

'No, they don't. Tell me. What happened?'

He picked up his glass and sat holding it. 'She threw herself off the roof of my block of flats this morning. From just above my study window. I saw her fall.'

The girl said nothing for a moment. She simply sat, looking down at the table in front of her. 'Threw herself? Are you sure?'

'She must have done. Unless somebody pushed her.'

'I didn't mean that.' The girl looked up. 'Did anyone else see it?'

'No. I live alone in the flat. My window looks out on a blank wall. There's an area yard in between.'

'You said you didn't know her.'

'That's true. Apparently she'd been sleeping up in the attic. Living rough.'

'The attic just above your flat?' The girl was looking at him searchingly and sceptically. 'Without you seeing her?'

'There's no reason why I should have. In any case I'd been holed up for a week writing an article. I'd hardly been out. She could have passed the front door a dozen times without my seeing her.'

'Then what's all this about a newspaper story?'

'I'm only curious.' He turned the cold glass between his fingers. 'I take it you knew her pretty well?'

'Well enough to be able to tell you you're wasting your time. There was nothing in Rosamond's life that would be worth a quarter of a column in any newspaper. She was a perfectly ordinary kid from a perfectly ordinary home. She was – a bit unfortunate, that's all. Nothing very unusual, nothing very dramatic. A little sad, a little sordid perhaps. But decidedly not newsworthy.'

'Why not let me be the judge of that?'

She shook her head. 'I read newspapers. I know the kind of thing you people like to print.' She took a sip of orange juice. 'By the way, you haven't told me your name.'

'Paul Marriott.'

'Gail Canning,' she said.

He put his glass down slowly and looked at her. 'St George's Yard. The girl with the purples.' He was gratified to see a faintly startled look come into her face. 'I ran into a young man called John Aubrey this evening,' he went on. 'He'd come looking for Rosamond Clay and we had a long talk.'

'John Aubrey?' She seemed to have recovered her composure. 'That must be the boy she was living with.'

'If you can call it living.'

'Look . . .' She sat back in her chair. 'You think I'm a drug pusher or something, is that it?'

'According to Aubrey, you were keeping Rosamond Clay supplied with purple hearts. But you weren't giving her quite enough of them, and you threatened to cut the supply off altogether if she didn't go back to see her doctor.'

40

'That's perfectly true. I was trying to help her. It seemed the only way of doing it.' Gail Canning paused. 'She'd taken against the doctor. She'd become totally unmanageable. Purple hearts were the only thing she wanted.'

Paul sat thinking for a few seconds. 'From what Aubrey told me, she must have been pretty sick. If she'd consulted a doctor, I imagine he would have put her straight into hospital.'

There was a brief silence. The girl picked up her glass and put it down again. 'She wasn't so bad at first. It was only later she started going downhill. Seriously so. I'm very sorry she's dead. I did my best . . . All right?'

He said nothing for a moment. It was far from all right, he thought. The way Aubrey had described the scene in the mews flat, it hadn't been a bit like Gail Canning's version. She had laughed at Rosamond when the girl had said she was going to kill herself. Hardly the way for a friend to behave.

'Rosamond was very sick.' Gail reached for her handbag on the table. 'Even if there were a story in it for your paper, I'm sure she wouldn't want it told. May we leave it like that?'

He shrugged. 'Very well.'

They both got up and went out of the pub.

They crossed King's Road without speaking. Then, as they covered the few yards to the Lord Kitchener, she said, 'Where's John Aubrey now? Still living in your attic?'

'Last seen heading for Shepherd's Bush. He said he'd found a new pad there.'

She merely nodded. Paul looked round at her. 'He seemed to think Rosamond Clay was desperately frightened of something.'

They reached the pub. She stopped, put her hand on the door and looked round at him. He could hear the muffled thumping and wailing of the music inside. 'God,' she said.

'What?'

'You mean, who.'

'I thought you said God.'

'I did.' Her expression was perfectly serious. ' "The Hound of Heaven". You know? "I fled him down the arches of the years; I fled him down the labyrinthine ways of my own mind . . ." Rosamond was pursued by God. She talked about it all the time. She was made. Incurably mad.'

She opened the door and for a second the rock music came blasting through it. Then she disappeared into the darkness beyond, the door closing behind her. Paul stood a moment, the white eyes on the windows staring sightlessly at him. Then he turned and started slowly back to where he had parked the car.

It was after midnight when he went to bed. He didn't feel like sleep. Lying in the dark room, he thought about John Aubrey; the gentle and soft-spoken young man living with the mad girl in the attic. Rosamond sitting on the roof, hepped up with Pernod and purple hearts, frantically scribbling down her verses before she hurled herself into the void. An owl hooted from among the trees in Bramham Gardens, a ghostly sound in the stillness. The gardener in the square had once told him that there had been owls living there since his grandfather's time. He thought suddenly of Fred. Fred's last visit to the scullery had been the shortest he could remember. He wondered vaguely what could have driven him away; what for that matter had brought him here in the first place; what outlandish freak of chance, what unimaginable accident of nature, had caused a young Edwardian boy, once hungry for life, to wait through nearly eighty long years in an empty scullery for a dead serving maid. He turned uneasily between the sheets.

The owl hooted again, balefully, at the London night. It was strange to think that the Edwardian boy's parents had lain together in this very room. She carrying her child. He imagined her suddenly, getting up from her bed, burdened and sleepless. He saw her walking the long empty corridors of the apartment, listening to the owl, carrying a ghost in her womb.

Looking in his AA book next morning, he found Tarrybridge. Tarrybridge, Sussex; half-way between Burgess Hill and Brighton.

After the breathless heat of London it was a relief to be driving through the countryside, the trees heavy with their late summer leaves, the cornfields cropped and bare after an early harvest. 'The speechless fields.' Rosamond Clay's notebook lay in his pocket. He had read the verses again over breakfast that morning and already knew some of them by heart.

His interest in poetry went back to the years when he had studied litera ure at Cambridge and had himself written highly experimental verse, for the most part expressions of anger and protest in the style of Allen Ginsberg. It had been the era of Suez and the Campaign for Nuclear Disarmament. More than twenty years ago now, he reflected wryly. As a young reporter covering the provinces for a news agency, he had continued to submit work to *avant-garde* magazines; he still had some of the rejection slips. Perhaps it was as well that Fleet Street should have claimed him, that he should have forgotten his literary aspirations in the struggle to become one of the country's leading crime reporters. He felt no bitterness about this. Better to be a successful journalist than a failed creative writer. He was a man who liked to win.

His thoughts came back to Rosamond Clay. He didn't believe that her verses were the product of a deranged mind. Though one at least had been prophetic of her fate, they had clearly not been written by the girl John Aubrey and Gail Canning had described. Aubrey had suggested that she had put them down from memory. They belonged, then, to an earlier though still quite recent period of her life; to the time before madness had so suddenly and inexplicably overtaken her. Aubrey was clearly a more reliable witness than Gail Canning; and he had said nothing about Rosamond being obsessed by God; he had only insisted that she had been frightened out of her senses in some unaccountable fashion. Yet he couldn't rid his mind of what Gail Canning had said to him outside the Lord Kitchener. It had been this more than anything else that had decided him to continue his search for the missing pieces in the girl's life. Gail Canning's remark about Rosamond being pursued by God had seemed to have a curious ring of truth. It wasn't the kind of thing anyone would make up. He frowned to himself. For the life of him he couldn't equate the ideas of the God-haunted Rosamond and the girl living on Pernod and purple hearts, rambling incoherently about a mysterious Music Room. It was obvious that Gail Canning had much to hide; and Aubrey had been less than frank. The more he pondered the matter, the more convinced he became that Rosamond Clay had been the victim of some conspiracy.

He drove through Hayward's Heath then out into the country again, past the broad farmlands and rolling hills of the South Downs.

> Black rooks
> Adorn
> The speechless fields.
> Like iron nails
> Their stillness
> Pins
> The living mind
> To horror
> Of the sky's indifference.
> With absolute authority
> Their nothingness

Prompts panic
Dream-awake
To scarecrow consciousness
Of the deadly
Final
Falling
Patient
Void.

Turning off the Brighton road, he entered Tarrybridge. From the local newsagent he learned that the Clays' house was a quarter of a mile away on the road to Steyning.

The house was quite large, built Georgian-style, with a spacious garden at the front. There was a Volvo station waggon parked outside the garage. The Clays were evidently well-to-do.

Opening a wrought iron gate, he walked up the garden to the door and knocked. It was opened after a moment by a tall grey-haired man wearing an open-necked shirt and a pair of baggy corduroy trousers. His face was drawn-looking and colourless.

'Mr Clay?' Paul said.

'Yes.' The voice sounded rather distant and uncertain.

'My name's Paul Marriott. I'm very sorry indeed to trouble you at a time like this. But it's about your daughter, Rosamond.'

'Rosamond . . .' The man stood staring at him for a moment through a pair of grey unfocused eyes. He put his hand up a little gropingly and took hold of the edge of the door, rather as a blind man would. 'I see . . . You're not from the police?'

'No.'

'We had them here yesterday.' He said this as if he were referring to something that had happened fifty years ago. For a long moment he stood, still holding on to the edge of the door. Then he took a pace backward. 'Well, you'd better come in.'

Paul entered. Mr Clay closed the door and led him along the hall. A large bowl of chrysanthemums stood on an oak table in front of a gilt Italian mirror. They passed through an archway hung with horse brasses and Paul found himself in the living room: chintz-covered furniture and chintz curtains; roses this time in another bowl; a smell of cut flowers. Seated on a sofa in front of him was a frail-looking woman with red hair. She might have been about forty-five and Paul could see at once the likeness to Rosamond: the same green eyes, the same delicately pointed chin.

'Elizabeth,' Mr Clay said, 'this is Mr – ah . . .'

'Marriott. Paul Marriott.'

'It's about Rosamond,' the man said with an odd emphasis in his voice that Paul couldn't immediately interpret.

'Oh . . .' The woman gestured to a chair. 'Won't you please sit down?'

Paul went and sat. 'I should explain that I live at Earls Court Mansions,' he said. 'Where – the accident happened.'

'You knew our daughter?' Elizabeth Clay asked, a pathetic eagerness in her face.

'Well, no,' Paul replied. He wondered what the police had told the couple. Perhaps they had spared them the more sordid details of Rosamond's last days. 'But I happened to pick up something belonging to her. I wanted to return it to you.' He produced the notebook from his pocket. 'Some verses she wrote. I read them, I hope you don't mind. I thought they were very remarkable.'

There was a brief pause. The man and the woman were both staring at the little book in Paul's hand.

'There was only one book?' Mr Clay asked rather suddenly.

'Why, yes.'

For a moment the Clays were silent. Paul was puzzled.

There was a distinct, unexplainable atmosphere of tension in the room.

'You see, Rosamond usually carried a whole lot of notebooks with her,' Mrs Clay said in a hurried, nervous voice. 'Sometimes a dozen or more .We . . .' She caught her husband's eye and fell si'ent.

Mr Clay came forward and took the book from Paul. Without looking at it, he slipped it into the drawer of a bureau near by. 'It was very good of Mr Marriott to go to all this trouble,' he said to his wife in a faintly reprimanding tone. 'Extraordinarily kind.' He turned to Paul. 'We're most grateful to you.'

'You say you didn't know Rosamond?' Mrs Clay asked after a moment.

'No . . .' The next, very obvious, question remained unasked. Paul let it hang in the air for a few seconds. Then he said, 'I spent a little time with the police yesterday. They were going through your daughter's belongings and I picked up the book. I was so struck by the verses, I decided to read them before returning them to you.' There was another pause, the man and the woman regarding him searchingly and sceptically. 'She had a unique talent,' he went on. 'I was curious to know if she'd written more.'

'Oh, yes. She wrote a great many poems.' It was Mrs Clay who answered. She spoke a little cautiously, keeping one eye on her husband as if she were afraid of saying too much. 'She used to win prizes for them at her convent. Then she had some published in a little magazine.'

'Recently?'

'No, it was before she left home.'

'I see.' Paul got to his feet. 'I don't want to bother you with this now. But if it were possible to get more of her verses together some time, I'd like to try to interest a publisher. I believe they should be read.' He looked at Mrs Clay. 'You mentioned other notebooks. If they were still in London, if she'd left them with friends perhaps, I

47

could always arrange to collect them.'

'We know nothing about Rosamond's London friends,' Mr Clay said in an unexpectedly loud voice. 'We had very little contact with her over the past year. We know nothing about the kind of life she led, where she lived or who she associated with.' He threw a look of anguished appeal at his wife. 'If there were any other notebooks, we've heard nothing of them.'

Paul looked quickly from one to the other. Mr Clay's words had sounded almost like a prepared statement. Mrs Clay was fidgeting with her hands; she seemed on the point of bursting into tears. Watching them, Paul suddenly realised something. The two people were not only grief-stricken. They were frightened.

Just then he heard someone enter the room. Turning his head, he felt a momentary shock. A young girl wearing jeans and a T-shirt was standing in the archway; she had short red hair and a pair of wideawake green eyes set far apart in a vivacious, elfin face. It took him a second to realise that she was much younger than Rosamond, hardly more than sixteen.

'Oh, I'm sorry . . .' she said, her eyes resting with frank curiosity on Paul.

'Darling, this is Mr Marriott,' Mrs Clay said. 'Our daughter Nicola.'

The girl continued to regard Paul for a few seconds; the expression of deep interest in her gaze made him feel a little uncomfortable. Then she turned to her mother. 'I was looking for my guitar book. I wanted to pack it, but it doesn't matter now.' She went out of the room, giving Paul a swift look over her shoulder as she did so.

'She's going back to school this afternoon,' Mrs Clay said. 'We thought it better.'

Paul got to his feet. 'I won't keep you any longer. It was very good of you to see me.'

'Not at all. Good-bye, Mr Marriott,' the woman said.

48

'I'll take you to the gate.' Her husband started towards the arch.

Paul followed him along the hall and through the front door. They walked down the garden path in silence. Mr Clay opened the gate and paused, reaching for a hoe that was leaning against the post. He turned to Paul, hesitated and said, 'I've been doing a bit, you see. I've always been a keen gardener, and it's best to keep yourself busy.'

'Yes, indeed,' Paul said.

Curiously, Mr Clay seemed reluctant all at once to let him go. He stood for a few seconds gazing about the garden. 'It's the weeds, you know. Let them loose, they do untold damage.' With a rather quick movement of his head, he looked round at Paul again. For the first time his weak grey eyes seemed to come to focus on his visitor. 'They strangle the young plants,' he said. 'They poison the earth. You have to keep them down. You simply have to. It's no use chopping them off . . .' He looked at the bright blade of the hoe; a flush of colour had come into his pale cheeks. 'You have to dig right down. You have to get them out by the roots. Uproot them before they run rife and destroy everything.'

Paul nodded. It was clear that the man was desperately trying to tell him something. Before he could think of a suitable reply, Mr Clay started to walk away, hoe in hand, quickly up the garden.

Paul stood watching him for a few seconds, then he let himself out through the gate and went to where his car was parked. He was about to open the door when a voice from near by said softly, 'Mr Marriott . . .'

He looked round to see Nicola Clay coming from behind the car. She stopped very close to him, her wide green eyes anxious and questioning. 'I heard you talking to Mummy and Daddy – about Rosamond . . .'

'Yes?'

'She killed herself, didn't she? She said she was going to.'

49

'She said so? When?'

'The last time I saw her. In London. On my way home from Wimbledon, from school. She told me she was going to commit suicide.'

'Nicola! Are you there?' Mr Clay's voice came from the garden.

'But why?' Paul asked.

'She had this God thing.'

'Nicola!' They could hear the man's footsteps on the path.

'What God thing?'

'Something to do with Bloomsbury,' the girl said quickly. 'A place in Bloomsbury . . .'

The gate opened with a slight clatter. Mr Clay said, 'Nicola – will you please come in this minute!'

The girl hesitated fractionally, giving Paul a brief helpless look. Then she walked away into the garden. The man closed the gate and stood looking in a faintly alarmed fashion through the bars at Paul.

Paul opened the car door, climbed in behind the wheel and drove off.

Looking for God in Bloomsbury. He felt slightly foolish as he walked along Great Russell Street that afternoon. The heat had grown more intense; London suffocating under a pewter-coloured sky. His task, he told himself, was well-nigh hopeless. He hadn't the faintest idea what he was searching for. From under the plane trees of Bloomsbury Square the statue of Charles James Fox looked over at the glaring white terraces of Bedford Place. Ahead of him, the soot-black, pigeon-stained British Museum; the crowds of tourists splashing the forecourt with colour.

He turned into Bury Place, one of the little streets opposite the Museum. There was a shop on the corner displaying piles of tartan shawls and blankets; a small travel agency; a wholesale printers; a bookshop and a snack bar. Near the bottom of the street he paused, looking at a sign on the wall of a modest cream-painted building. 'The Radha Krishna Temple. Society for Krsihna Consciousness. Visitors welcome from 4 a.m. to 9 p.m.' It seemed hardly likely that this could have anything to do with Rosamond Clay. Nonetheless he climbed the short flight of steps and opened the door.

The hallway beyond was narrow and perfectly bare save for two large fire-extinguishers standing in the middle of the floor. He waited a moment, then a man appeared from the end of the hall: a young shaven-headed Indian wearing saffron robes and carrying a little canvas bag round his neck. Negotiating the fire-extinguishers, he came forward with a smile on his round and slightly pock-marked face. 'Hare Krishna,' he said.

'Good afternoon,' Paul replied. 'I wonder if you can help me. I'm a journalist. I'm writing an article about the kind of religious groups young people are joining nowadays. Particularly the oriental faiths. I'd very much like to know what you do here. Perhaps you could spare me a few minutes.'

'Of course, with pleasure,' the Indian said. 'But I must ask you to take off your shoes.'

Paul obediently removed his shoes and placed them by the skirting board. The Indian led him past the fire-extinguishers and up a flight of stairs. On the landing above a blonde girl in a sari was operating a hand-turned Gestetner machine. The Indian gestured to a doorway and they went into one of the front rooms. Here in the middle of the floor was another fire-extinguisher. Two tables stood against the window, one covered with a red cloth, the other with a purple cloth; on the purple cloth was an oversize Thermos flask and a bowl of bananas.

Paul and the Indian sat down facing each other on low cane chairs. 'We are practitioners of bhakati yoga,' the Indian said without preamble, 'according to the *Bhagavad Gita*, our book of spiritual wisdom dating from Vedic times a thousand years before Christ. Through the

51

Bhagavad Gita you are brought directly in touch with the Lord Krishna.'

'Who is Krishna?' Paul asked.

'God has many names,' the Indian told him. 'When we speak of Krishna, you should remember that this is not a sectarian name. Krishna means "all pleasure" or the "all attractive". Krishna, the supreme Lord, is the well-spring of pleasure, the spirit that guides and informs all our activities. Our consciousness seeks happiness because we are part of the Lord. The Lord is always happy, and if we identify our activities with his, we will partake of his happiness. This is the purpose of bhakati yoga.' The Indian took a string of wooden beads from the bag around his neck and fingered them. 'When a man claims allegiance to some particular faith, this is not eternal. A man can change his faith. Such changeable faith, therefore, is not religion. However, the Hindu, the Moslem or the Christian is always a servant. So the faith is not the religion. Service is the religion. We call it Sanatana-darma. That which cannot be changed. Liquidity cannot be taken from water, heat cannot be taken from fire. So Sanatana-darma cannot be taken from living entities which have no birth and which never die, which continue to live after the destruction of the material body, just as they lived before its formation.'

At this moment the girl in the sari came in carrying a paper plate and a paper cup. As she proffered these to Paul the Indian said, 'Prasada, the remains of food offered to the Lord. It is spiritual and purifying. The food is Krishna himself. You should eat it all or you will be showing disrespect to Krishna.'

'Thank you,' Paul said as the girl left the room.

'It is an ancient Vedic recipe,' the Indian explained, 'consisting of fruit and vegetables. What we call food in the mode of goodness, quite distinct from such untouchable things as meat and liquor.'

Paul nodded. He had had a late lunch on his way back

from Tarrybridge. The paper cup appeared to contain rice, a thing he disliked. He swallowed some and said, 'You've opened a temple here, you must have a lot of English devotees. What are they, mostly young people?'

'Yes, they are nearly all young. We also have a farm community in Letchmore Heath not far from London.'

'What happens there?' Paul asked.

'Our disciples work the farm, practise bhakati and study the *Bhagavad Gita*.'

'The notice outside says you welcome visitors from 4 a.m. It seems you follow a very strict regime.'

The Indian smiled. 'We practise austerity – cleanliness, simplicity, celibacy and non-violence as a way to knowledge and enlightenment. In this way we are liberated from the mode of ignorance. The results of this mode are madness, indolence and sleep which imprison the soul. We purify our activities in order to draw our minds away from material entanglements. This is the essence of what we call bhakati, or devotional service.'

While the Indian went on talking, Paul struggled to get through the sacred food. He was by now reasonably certain that he had drawn a blank. He could see nothing sinister in the picture of Rosamond Clay farming and meditating among a group of saffron-robed drop-outs in Letchmore Heath; Rosamond in this little room listening to the gentle Indian seated by the fire-extinguisher. Whatever she had happened upon in Bloomsbury, it could hardly have been this. With relief, he put down the empty plate and cup.

The Indian rose from the chair. 'If you like, I will show you the temple.'

They left the room and as Paul padded down the stairs in his stocking feet, the Indian said, 'The purpose of life is to understand why we are suffering. One should ask, Where am I from? Where am I going? When these questions are awakened in the mind of a sane man, then he can understand *Bhagavad Gita*. Out of many, many human beings *Bhagavad Gita* is directed to the one who seeks to understand the mysteries of birth, disease, old age and death which haunt us all.'

They walked along the hallway. The Indian opened a door and they entered the temple, a long room filled with benches. At the far end was an altar which looked for all the world like something out of a fun fair. Covered with bright red cloth, it displayed two mannikin figures: Krishna and perhaps a disciple. Standing about two feet high, they were dressed in white silken robes studded with a mass of artificial jewels, their wildly elaborate head-dresses of lace and tulle liberally sprinkled with sequins and pieces of diamanté. The altar was strewn with rose petals; on the floor stood a bowl of food and a glass water jug. A little to one side, the girl in the white sari was moving back and forth carrying an incense burner and chanting ceaselessly to the two figures: 'Hare Krishna, Hare Krishna, Krishna, Krishna, Hare, Hare. Hare Rama, Hare Rama, Hare, Hare.'

The Indian had got down on his knees. Paul had compromised by folding his hands in front of him and lowering his head reverently. They remained like that for some minutes, then the Indian rose and led him out into the hall again. While Paul was putting on his shoes, the man said, 'The material world has been described as *asvattah*, a tree which has its roots upward. We have experience of this when we stand by a lake. We can see in the reflection that the tree's roots are upward and its branches downward. So this material world is a reflection of the spiritual world, just as the reflection of the tree from the bank is seen to be upside down. This material world is like a shadow. In a shadow there cannot be any substance, yet we can understand from the shadow that there is a substance. In the reflection of the spiritual world there is no happiness, but in the spiritual world itself there is real happiness.'

They went down the hall together. The Indian opened

the door. 'Man is both flesh and spirit,' he said. 'Hare Krishna.'

Both flesh and spirit. Paul came out of Bury Place, walked along Bloomsbury Way and took the next turning into Museum Street. It yielded a publishing house, some more bookshops, a silversmith's and an espresso bar. There were two small side streets running off at right angles and he searched these. Little Russell Street produced a hairdresser's, a seedy-looking block of flats, the back of a church and the staff entrance to the Kingsley Hotel. Gilbert Place contained a few obscure company offices and another block of flats; the rest of the buildings were abandoned and apprently under compulsory purchase.

He found himself opposite the gold-spiked railings of the British Museum once more. Turning, he walked a few yards and started down Coptic Street. An empty building occupied most of the first block, refuse-filled rooms visible through the grimy windows, dusty telephone books on the floor, a 'To Let' sign leaning upside down against a wall. There was a petrol station with a bomb-site parking area beyond, a pizzeria, a doctor's consulting room, a snack bar and the purple-painted facade of an Indian emporium. Next came a gloomy little shop, dust collecting on pieces of oriental statuary in the window. Further on, a flight of steps led up to a faded yellow door. Fixed to the door was a small brass plate which read: 'The Regiment of God. Fifth Church of the Eternal Spirit. Registered Office.' The place looked unprepossessing: a half-drawn blind over one window; in the other, secured by a single piece of Sellotape, a curling red, white and blue poster carrying the exhortation 'FIGHT FOR GOD'.

The door stood ajar. Paul climbed the steps and went inside. To his right, the hallway opened directly into a reception area furnished with a table and a few chairs. There was nobody to be seen; in the hot silence a fly buzzed and beat its head against the window pane under the 'FIGHT FOR GOD' poster. Going into the reception area, he looked about him. A Union Jack and an American flag hung from poles against the far wall; between them was a large photograph of a United States general, his expression grimly set, a pair of black glittering eyes looking out from deep cavernous sockets. 'General Lee Anderton' according to the gold lettering at the foot of the heavy black frame. He moved to the table where some books were displayed. They were all from the General's hand, solid-looking in red, white and blue jackets. He read the titles: *America and the Second Covenant, I Spoke to God, God's Will and My Part in It, Combat Mission God. How I Was Briefed.* He had turned his head and was looking speculatively at the portrait again when he heard the rattle of a mop and pail from the hallway. Going out, he saw a woman in an overall preparing to wash down the linoleum floor. She had a florid, rather belligerent-looking face and wore a bandanna tied round her hair. 'You looking for someone?' she asked.

'I came to inquire about the church.'

The woman brought the mop down with a loud splash on the floor and looked behind her. 'Mr Skeggs!' she shouted. 'Somebody's come to inquire!'

Showing no more concern, she devoted her energies to the floor, thrusting vigorously with the mop and sending water swilling over the linoleum towards Paul's feet. He waited for what seemed a long time. The woman plunged her mop into the pail again and went on with her swabbing. Then a man appeared from the back of the hallway. He was about fifty, sparely built and erect of bearing; he had short grey hair, a broken nose and a pair of large ears sticking out from the sides of his head. A figure you would be more likely to see in a gymnasium than in a place of religion. Wearing a grey flannel shirt and a pair of neatly pressed navy blue trousers, he came purposefully past the cleaning woman to give Paul a thin-lipped smile. 'I'm sorry, sir,' he said briskly. 'I didn't hear you come in. Step this way, I'll give you some of our literature.'

56

Paul followed him into the reception area. 'Do you get many callers here?' he asked.

'Quite a few, sir.' Skeggs was taking some pamphlets from a shelf. 'Of course it's a bit slack now, being holiday time.'

'Have you been going very long?'

'About six months. The First Church was founded by General Anderton after the Vietnam War.' The man paused. 'May I ask what brought you here, sir? Was it a recommendation?'

'No,' Paul said. 'I happened to be passing and saw your poster.'

Skeggs looked over at the window. The fly was still trying to get out. He didn't move for a moment; he simply stood with his eyes fixed on the curling poster. The only sound in the room was the buzzing of the fly. Then he turned back to the shelf, giving Paul another of his brief, thin smiles. 'We rely a lot on recommendations, you see. People pass the word along. It's how we get most of our new members.' He selected some more pamphlets, then came and presented them to Paul. 'They're all written by the General himself, sir. Then there's our newspaper. I've given you a copy of that. They'll tell you a great deal about us. Or if you wanted to buy one of the General's books, they retail at £5.95.'

'No, I think these will do for the moment,' Paul said. 'Thank you.'

Skeggs walked with him to the front door. 'We're holding our weekly prayers meeting and address at St Catherine's Hall this evening, sir. Six-fifteen. If you care to come along, you'd be very welcome.'

'St Catherine's Hall? Where's that?'

'Kemble Street. The bottom of Kingsway.'

Paul nodded.

'I shall look forward to seeing you, sir.' Skeggs opened the door and Paul went down the steps.

He had now searched Bloomsbury from end to end. The

Regiment of God seemed hardly more suspect than the Krishna Temple. He was half-inclined to go home. But he was persistent by nature. A visit to the prayer meeting would cost him nothing, and he was in any case just a little curious.

There was a pub on the next corner and he went in. Ordering a drink, he sat down and leafed through the pamphlets. Their tone was curiously outdated. If God had spoken to the General, then he had spoken with the voice of Senator McCarthy. It was the old reds-under-the-bed cold war paranoia of the 1950s. The enemy was everywhere, entrenched in the schools, the universities, the labour unions and the mass media. The Western world was a rotten fruit ready to fall and only General Anderton, the inspired leader of a new militant puritanism, could save us all from the ultimate evil of Soviet domination.

Laying aside the pamphlets, he turned his attention to the newspaper. It was called *Bastion*. Tabloid in format, it ran to eight pages, sold for fifteen pence and carried no advertising. The lead story was entitled 'God's Scenario'. It explained how God had been manipulating the forces of history during the past few decades, as much in our domestic affairs as in places like the Middle East and Vietnam, so as to bring about the fulfilment of his aims. The time was now approaching when, through the instrument of General Anderton, God would marshal the forces of the free world against the Devil who was currently masquerading under the guise of international communism. The appeal was exclusively to youth. It was the young, wearied of the excesses of the permissive age – experiencing 'the great disgust' – who would shave their heads, dedicate themselves to order, services and discipline and, 'built foursquare in body and soul', flock to the ever-swelling ranks of the Regiment of God.

The emblem of the regiment, conspicuous on the masthead of the journal, was a mailed fist. Paul sighed and finished his drink. Gathering up the literature, he left the pub and headed for Kingsway.

St Catherine's Hall, with its *art-nouveau* frontage of peeling stucco, looked rather like an old-time cinema. A large poster hung in a glass-fronted case by the entrance: 'God Cares about Britain. Do You? Join the Regiment of God. Fight for the Homeland You Love and Cherish'. And beneath, written with a felt pen, 'Prayer Meeting and Address tonight. 6.15'.

Passing through the doors, Paul found himself in a small and ill-lit foyer. Skeggs, wearing a dark suit for the occasion, was standing behind a table near the half-curtained entrance to the hall. Picking up a Roneoed hymn sheet, he gave it to Paul. 'Go right on in, sir,' he said affably. 'We're about to start.'

The hall was as depressingly dim as the foyer, the walls chocolate brown, the windows composed of red and green diamonds of stained glass. Rows of collapsible chairs faced a small stage backed by a dark red curtain of dusty velvet. There was nothing on the stage except a school easel draped with a faded banner, a relic perhaps of some long-forgotten religious crusade: 'Jehovah Is Thy Lord'. To the right, just beneath the stage, stood an ancient harmonium, the keyboard illuminated by a bare electric light bulb slung over the back of a music stand. The attendance was poor: a mere twenty people scattered thinly about the auditorium. They were all middle-aged and rather shabby-looking, the kind of lonely eccentrics Paul imagined you would see at a meeting of the Flat Earth Society.

He found a place in one of the middle rows. Behind him a large crimson-faced man sat breathing heavily and fanning himself with a copy of *Dalton's Weekly*. In front of him three elderly ladies in flower print dresses were whispering earnestly among themselves. To his right, one chair away, a tall woman in a long knitted dress sat staring at a shoebox on her knee. She had a very white, curiously ravaged-looking face and wore a grubby linen hat perched on the top of her head. The lid of the shoebox, Paul noticed with mild concern, was pierced with holes. Consulting the Roneoed sheet in his hand, he noticed that the meeting was to begin with the singing of 'Land of Hope and Glory'.

After a few minutes Skeggs appeared. He came down the aisle, removing the waterproof covering from a Union Jack on the end of a pole. Crossing to the harmonium, he balanced the flag precariously against it and sat down. 'You will kindly rise for the singing,' he said in aloud, unctuous voice.

There was a clattering of chairs as everyone got up. The harmonium gave a loud asthmatic wheeze. Skeggs then launched into a rendering of 'Land of Hope and Glory' that would have made Elgar turn in his grave. His knowledge of the instrument was rudimentary; but what he lacked in skill he made up for in sheer verve. If there was any response from the gathering, this was entirely drowned by the man with the crimson face. He had a booming bass voice that would have filled the Albert Hall and he sang with an enthusiasm and an extravagance of feeling that matched the wild abandon of the harmonium player. Paul stood silent, catching the full blast of the man's voice together with an overpowering smell of stale beer and onions. There was to be little relief. 'Land of Hope and Glory' was followed almost immediately by three verses of 'Onward Christian Soldiers'. Paul looked round at the woman in the knitted dress. She was standing perfectly still, seemingly oblivious of what was going on, her gaze fixed on the shoebox in her hands. Finally, after two false starts, Skeggs managed to hit the right key for Blake's 'Jerusalem'.

> I will not cease from mental fight,
> Nor shall my sword sleep in my hand,
> Till we have built Jerusalem
> In England's green and pleasant land.

There was silence at last. Everybody sat down. Skeggs remained at the harmonium, his hands resting on his lap.

For a long time nothing happened. Then Paul heard footsteps coming down the aisle. A young man appeared, heading for the stage. He climbed some steps by the proscenium and faced the hall. He was in his early twenties and wore a neat grey suit; his fair hair was cropped close to his head and there was a set and earnest expression on his sharp, clean-cut features. 'Ladies and gentlemen, good evening,' he said. 'May I ask you all please to get to your feet?'

The chairs clattered and scraped again as everyone rose. The speaker stood perfectly still, his hands at his sides, looking over the heads of the gathering. 'We are going to spend two minutes in silent prayer,' he announced in his clear, authoritative voice. 'We are going to ask God to look down in mercy upon this country of ours, upon Great Britain, our glorious and beloved homeland.'

Out of the corner of his eye Paul saw the woman in the knitted dress carefully lifting the lid of the shoebox. He turned his head. With a superior and faintly conspiratorial smile on her face, she was gazing downward. The box was full of live snails, nearly a dozen of them, trailing their slimy courses over a bed of cabbage leaves.

'I want each of you, in your own way, to ask God to come to the help of our beleaguered and sorely threatened nation. I want you to ask him to give each and every one of you the strength to fight the enemy, the Beast that lurks in our very midst. For we are the instruments of God, and it only through him that we will prevail against the Beast.' Folding his hands in front of him, he lowered his cropped blond head as if he were performing a drill movement. 'Let us pray,' he said.

The two minutes seemed very long to Paul, the woman still staring at her snails, the man behind him breathing his beer and onion breath.

At last the speaker looked up. 'Now will you kindly be

seated? he said.

Paul sat down. The woman put the lid back on her shoebox.

The young man walked a little way upstage and faced the auditorium again. After a moment he started to speak, more loudly now, as if he were addressing an audience twenty times the size of the little gathering. 'Stretch out your sickle and reap; for the harvest time has come, and the earth's crop is over-ripe. Hear, you who have ears to hear, what the Spirit says to his Churches!' He let a momentary silence pass. The woman in the knitted dress threw back her head and gave a clearly audible snigger. The speaker appeared to notice nothing. 'You have all read how the Devil was thrown down to earth and how he conferred his power upon the Beast. How the Beast opened its mouth in blasphemy against God. How the whole world went after the Beast in wondering admiration. Men worshipped the Devil because he had conferred his authority upon the Beast; they worshipped the Beast also and chanted, "Who is like the Beast? Who can fight against it?" You have read also of Babylon the Great, the mother of whores. How all nations drank deep of the fierce wine of her fornication and the kings of the earth committed fornication with her. How the foul corrosive poisons of her spirit spilled into every corner of the earth.' The young man paused and looked slowly round the hall. 'Do I have to name the Beast? Do I have to point my finger at Babylon the Great? You must know of what I am speaking. You must know what dire urgency, what fearful relevance these words have for us today.'

The Book of Revelation was quickly brought up to date by the young skinhead. What was Babylon but Moscow, the Beast but the menace of world Marxism? Carefully, and at some length, the speaker went on to explain how the agents of the Beast, with grim determination and consummate cunning, had succeeded in infiltrating every aspect of our lives, weakening our moral fibre and sowing havoc throughout the body politic.

Paul listened and pondered. He couldn't help but be impressed, and a little disturbed, by what he was witnessing. Here was no ordinary crank, no weekend orator, no ranting Sunday fascist. The speaker carried himself with an air of distinct authority, a cold and self-disciplined assurance, that was curiously troubling to see in one so young. There was a suggestion of restrained menace, something cobra-like and dangerous, about the blond preacher which, in spite of the extravangance of his oratory, made him seem a formidable and rather frightening figure.

'We must turn our backs upon our present rulers,' the speaker went on, 'when we see what they now call rule – to chaffer and bargain for power with the rabble. There is no greater misfortune in all man's fate than when the powerful of the earth are not also the First of Men. Then all grows false and warped and monstrous. And if, worst of all, they are the last of men, and more Beast than man – the price of the rabble rises and rises, and at length the rabble-voice says: "Behold, I am virtue!"' The young man paused again. The woman with the shoebox gave a little snort of derision. The passage had sounded to Paul like a quotation; it certainly wasn't biblical and he was at a loss to identify it. 'Let us have no illusions,' the speaker continued in his clear, chilling tones. 'We have already arrived at this very situation. Power in Great Britain today is no longer the monopoly of our so-called rulers. Side by side with the state we have a parallel apparatus controlled by revolutionaries whose avowed purpose is to destroy everything we cherish, whose foreign masters would drive freedom and justice for ever from this land. These men are the Devil's brood. They are the cohorts of darkness. This is the Beast come again to enslave, corrupt and befoul – to turn our blessed homeland into a Godless place in which free men will be forced to worship in their heavy chains the faceless idols of a foreign power. As St John exhorted his fellow Christians to withstand the onslaughts of paganism – so we, the soldiers of the Regiment of God, exhort you to take up arms against the heathen forces of international communism.' The crewcut figure in the grey suit came a little way downstage. 'I want you all to tell your friends – particularly the young among them – that they need no longer wait helpless and confused upon events. Tell them that there is now a rallying point: a bastion is being raised, an army is being assembled, to do battle against the forces of atheism and anarchy that have built a reeking Babylon in England's green and pleasant land. Tell them – these young people – that what we would demand of them is a return to Christian purity, a road back to God and sanity; a turning away from the squalid materialism of this age that has spurned patriotism, cast doubt on all traditions and made a mockery of moral values. What we need more than anything else at this moment is to recruit the courage and integrity of youth to the ranks of a new order. Tell them we are here, ready to receive them. For by the grace of heaven we have among us now one of the First of Men – General Lee Anderton, the founder and leader of this movement who has it from the very mouth of God that we shall triumph over our enemies. He who has come to lead us back to Christ, behind whom we must close our ranks and prepare to do battle against the Beast. "For great and marvellous are Thy ways, O Lord God, sovereign of all." '

The preacher fell silent, standing motionless at the foot of the stage. There was a slight stirring in the hall, people clearing their throats and gathering up shopping bags.

'Would anyone like to ask a question?' the man said.

There was a momentary pause. Then the woman with the shoebox rose to her feet. 'How is it you've never heard of the Venusians?' she demanded in a querulous voice. 'You must surely know that at this moment Jesus Christ is hard at work on the planet Venus preparing for his second coming.' Pulling her linen hat more firmly down on her head, she gave one of her contemptuous laughs. 'So you've absolutely nothing to worry about, young man. Master Aetherius has everything in hand.'

The grey-suited man looked round at Skeggs. Skeggs immediately addressed himself to the harmonium, pumped the pedals and launched into a fractured rendering of 'Abide With Me'.

The woman in the knitted dress came past Paul and started along the empty row of seats. The speaker had left the stage and was making his way up the aisle towards the exit. Paul, anxious to waylay him, got to his feet and headed after the woman. She had paused at the end of the row to let the speaker pass. Just as Paul reached her, she turned to him. 'Isn't it perfectly ridiculous?' she said. 'All he has to do is tune in to Mars Section Six like everybody else. Aetherius, Saint Goo-ling or anyone up there will tell him. Satellite Three has been in close orbit for days now . . .'

The blond man had disappeared through the exit door. 'Excuse me,' Paul said.

Pushing past the woman, he crossed the aisle. Several other people had already converged on the exit. By the time he reached the foyer there was no sign of the speaker.

He ran down the steps to the pavement in time to see the grey-clad figure walking quickly round the side of the hall. Setting off in pursuit, he reached the corner and stopped abruptly. The man was climing into a green MGB sports car, a girl seated at the wheel. The door slammed and the car shot past him, turned and headed towards Kingsway.

Paul stood on the pavement, looking after it. The woman in the knitted dress went by, smiling absently down at her cardboard box. For several seconds Paul didn't move, watching the MGB vanish into the traffic. The girl at the wheel was Gail Canning.

'Merlin's ticking,' David Plummer said to him in the news

room half an hour later. 'He's not interested in terrorists, North Sea oil rigs or any of that caper. He wants you to get stuck into the rabies story.' Plummer sank his teeth into a doughnut, bright crystals of sugar adhering to his thick lips. 'Apparently there's a vet in Calais specialises in giving knockout drops to our furry friends so people can carry them, sleeping peacefully in the bottoms of beach bags, past the coastguards at Folkestone. You could use it as a peg, unless something more newsworthy comes up.'

'Rabid man bites dog,' Paul suggested.

'The Customs and Excise people know about the vet. Talk to them. Talk to Eddie Campbell and anyone else you can think of. But Merlin wants to see it all in Saturday week's edition or he'll have your bollocks and mine.'

Paul waited until the News Editor had finished eating his doughnut and was wiping his mouth and fingers with a piece of Kleenex. 'Do we know anything about a religious sect called the Regiment of God?' he asked.

Plummer thought a moment. 'Barry Hellman was saying something to me about it not long ago. Why?'

Briefly Paul told him about Rosamond Clay's suicide, his visit to the family, to Coptic Street and St Catherine's Hall.

Plummer looked dubious. 'Not a lot to go on, is there? And you know how bloody sensitive these religious groups are. Have a word with Barry if you like. But remember Friday's your deadline on the other thing.'

Paul nodded and got to his feet. Leaving Plummer scribbling on the dummy for tomorrow's front page, he crossed the news room. The place was beginning to fill up, messengers hurrying between the desks, the orchestration of typewriter keys and telephone bells so familiar to his ears that he scarcely noticed it.

He found Barry Hellman at the far end of the room, sitting at his desk and staring at his typewriter as if he had never seen one before. He was a highly conscientious young man of about twenty-seven with an unruly mop of

66

hair and a lean, haggard face. 'Hello, Paul,' he said. 'How's bribery and corruption?'

'Flourishing.' Paul leaned his hands on the desk. 'David tells me you did a story on a religious sect called the Regiment of God not long ago.'

'There was no story,' Hellman told him. 'It died the death.'

'What happened?'

'Well, let's see . . .' The reporter reached for his note-book and started leafing back through the pages. 'It was the end of August. I took a phone call from a woman called Mrs Tendler. She told me she wanted to make a complaint about the sect and asked for our help. It seems her eighteen-year-old son – Jack his name is – had joined them about six months before and gone off on some kind of training course.'

'A training course? Where?'

'She wasn't sure. She thought somewhere in Berkshire. Anyway she'd heard nothing from him for a long time. Then one day a friend of his turned up at the house, a young man called Bill Adams. He'd run into Jack in a Chelsea pub where they both used to work. Adams said he hardly recognised the boy when he saw him. He was dirty, unshaven, half-starved, going round in a kind of daze. He didn't seem to know where he was or what had happened to him. All he'd say was that he'd been 'cast out', that he was 'living in a pit of darkness'. He owned a motor-bike and had been riding round the countryside for a week or more, living rough. Adams tried to persuade him to go home, but Jack Tendler said something to the effect that that was the last thing he'd ever do. He bor-rowed some money from Adams and left the pub. No one had seen him since.' Barry Hellman ran a hand through his hair. 'The poor woman sounded pretty desperate. She was convinced her son had been got at by the sect in some way. As it happened I had a pile of work on my desk, so I didn't go to see her until next morning. By then everything had changed. She wouldn't even let me through the front door. She seemed scared out of her wits, said her husband had forbidden her to talk to the press.'

'No explanation?'

'Only something about having to think of the other children. She said that if we dared print a word about her son, she'd sue us.' The reporter shrugged. 'Without the parents' co-operation, there wasn't much we could do. So we dropped the story.'

There was a brief silence. Paul stood deep in thought. A telephone rang unanswered on the desk beside him.

'I was a bit intrigued,' Hellman went on. 'So I spent the rest of the day beavering around, came up with quite a bit of stuff. For a start, their headquarters are listed in the telephone directory . . .'

'Coptic Street.'

'Yes. You've been there?'

Paul nodded. 'What about this man, General Anderton?'

'I got a run-down on him from the press office at the American Embassy,' Hellman said. 'The rest from a bloke I know on *Time* magazine.'

He turned the pages of his notebook again. Paul collected a chair from near by, pulled it up to the desk and sat down.

'Anderton was captured during the Vietnam war,' Hellman went on. 'He was given a pretty bad time by the communists. They wanted him to broadcast anti-American propaganda and he wouldn't play. It seems they tried just about everything, including a year in solitary confinement.' The young man looked round at Paul. 'Then, when he was released at the end of the war, he suddenly had a vision of God. In broad daylight, so the story goes, on the tarmac of Tokyo airport, God appeared before him as large as life.'

A girl came and put some papers on Hellman's desk. He glanced at them, then sat a moment fiddling with the shift key of his typewriter. 'God's message to the General was that he had to found seven churches dedicated to the overthrow of world communism. There are four going in the States now. The trend appears to be militant and activist. Most of the members are in their teens and early twenties. From the reports I've read, they seem to do a certain amount of good – emptying dustbins during strikes, looking after old people and that kind of thing. But there's another side to it. They've been accused of stirring up minor race riots in two American cities. More recently, a group of them helped picket a street in a predominantly white area of Chicago when a coloured family tried to move into the neighbourhood. There were scuffles with the police, kids carrying banners saying 'America Awake!', "Fight for God's Country" and suchlike. The usual crypto-fascist rubbish. Anderton, though, is said to have quite a charisma. He's putting something across and, in America at any rate, the movement is growing.'

'What about the church here?' Paul asked.

'On the surface it seems to be very low-key and quite respectable in a dotty kind of way. Registered as a charity and so on. Well, you've been there yourself.'

'I went to one of their meetings this evening,' Paul said. 'A rather terrifying young skinhead banging on about the communist menace and what God was going to do about it. A curious mixture of the Book of Revelations, reds-under-the-bed scaremongering and something else I couldn't quite identify. He seemed to have been pretty thoroughly indoctrinated. Somehow it didn't tie up with Coptic Street.'

Hellman sat back and frowned. 'I don't know. If they've got a training establishment in Berkshire or anywhere else, they're certainly keeping very quiet about it.'

Paul thought a moment. 'Could you give me the Tendlers' address?' he asked

'Out in Islington.' Hellman consulted his notebook.

'Thirty-eight Cordoba Villas. Off Caledonian Road, a few minutes walk from King's Cross.'

Cordoba Villas was a street of seedy-looking terrace houses with a brick Gothic church at one end and a breaker's yard full of derelict cars at the other. A crowd of kids were playing noisily in front of the yard, a burning pile of rubbish shimmering the air behind them. Half-way along the street a tall West Indian in a garish beach shirt was leaning against a brand-new Austin Allegro; the door was open, the radio playing at full volume, the man staring up at the hot white sky as if he could see angels.

As Paul climbed the steps of number thirty-eight a few of the children stopped playing and turned to watch him. He rang the bell. The door was opened by a woman in a pink housecoat. She had a long, rather horselike face and big teeth, her black hair dishevelled and hanging down to her shoulders.

'Mrs Tendler?'

'Yes.'

'I'm a newspaperman. A colleague of mine came to see you recently – about your son. I'm carrying out an investigation . . .'

'He's dead,' the woman said in a flat voice. 'Our Jack's dead.' She started to close the door.

Paul put his hand up and held it. 'Mrs Tendler, please – if you'd just tell me what happened . . .'

There was a sound of footsteps and a man appeared wearing a white singlet; his big coarse face was pink and blotchy-looking, a stubble of beard on his chin. 'What's this? You from the papers? Another reporter, are you?' For a moment he stood glaring at Paul in an anguished and belligerent fashion. 'Print any lies about our son, I'll have you in court. It was an accident, you understand? He was on his bike. Doing a ton . . .' The voice was hoarse and choked. 'Kid doing a ton. Had an accident. Ran his bike off the road. There's no more to it than that. Now go away and leave us in peace, for God's sake.' The door slammed in Paul's face.

Coming down the steps, he made his way back along the pavement. The West Indian was still watching the angels.

At the top of the street, on the corner of a small crescent by the church, was a youth club. It looked like a converted garage or workshop, a forecourt marked out for basketball, the old shed-like entranceway bricked in to leave a single door. Paul had noticed it on his way to the house. Now he paused, crossed the forecourt and went in.

There was nobody to be seen; a bare room with a concrete floor, a ping-pong table, a television set in the corner. From somewhere at the back of the building came the sound of hammering.

He crossed the room, passed through a doorway and found himself in a modest-sized hall, rows of chairs facing a stage at the far end. A man in shirtsleeves was standing on the stage, half-way up a step-ladder, a hammer in one hand, a string of bunting in the other. He watched inquiringly as Paul came down between the chairs.

'I was looking for the vicar,' Paul said.

The man got down from the steps, pushing a pair of hornrimmed spectacles back on to the bridge of his nose. He was about forty, with a dark, heavy face and a slightly harassed air. 'I'm the vicar,' he said. 'Donald Blythe.'

Paul climbed on to the stage and introduced himself. 'I was wondering if you happened to know a young man called Jack Tendler, lived down the way here at Cordoba Villas.'

'Why, yes. I knew him well. I know the family.' The vicar frowned. 'Just a minute, wasn't it your newspaper Mrs Tendler called a couple of weeks ago?'

'That's right,' Paul said.

The vicar nodded, nervously turning the hammer in his hand. 'She came and asked my advice about it. It seemed a good idea. I felt something should be done.'

'About this sect he joined? The Regiment of God?'

71

'Yes . . . Assuming they are responsible. One doesn't want to jump to conclusions. But what else is there to think?'

'I was a little puzzled,' Paul said. 'When our reporter went to see Mrs Tendler, she turned him away.'

'That was Harry Tendler.' The Reverend Blythe put the hammer on the steps and went to pick up a string of bunting from the floor. 'Her husband. When she told him what she'd done, he was furious. He came here, accused me of interfering in his private affairs. There was quite a scene.'

'What did he say?'

'Principally that he didn't want his son's name in the newspapers because of the other children. They have a boy and a girl of fourteen and sixteen.'

'Was that the only reason? You don't think he was being intimidated?'

The vicar stood a moment, the garland of little paper flags in his hands, looking at Paul in surprise. 'I couldn't say. It didn't occur to me.' He came and hung the flags over the top of the steps. 'He was in a highly emotional state. Perhaps he *was* afraid. I don't know. I find the whole business utterly bewildering.'

Paul walked to the edge of the platform and looked down at the empty chairs. 'Tell me about Jack Tendler. What sort of boy was he?'

'Oh . . . A serious lad. A churchgoer like his mother and father. He was one of the boys who helped build this stage as a matter of fact. We have a pop group, you know. He used to play the guitar. Rather well.' The vicar picked up the hammer and stared at it. 'Plenty of brains. A bit of a dreamer. An idealist, I suppose. He bought that bike of his, used to go off on his own a lot.' The man looked up, pushing his spectacles back on his nose again. 'He didn't seem able to find himself after he left school. He didn't know what he wanted, went drifting from job to job. A bit of a worry in some ways.'

'You don't know how he came to join the sect?'

'No. The last I heard he was working in some Chelsea pub. Then he wrote to his parents saying he'd become a member of this new religious group. They came and asked me if I knew anything about them. I made a few inquiries but could find out very little. In a way, I wasn't displeased. I hoped it might be the answer to his problems.'

'Did you talk to this friend of his – Bill Adams?'

'Yes, he came to see me. He couldn't tell me any more than he'd already told Mrs Tendler. Jack had been through some terrible experience . . . something dire – something quite shattering. What it could have been, I've no idea.'

'Nor have I.' Paul crossed the stage. 'If you hear any more, from the Tendlers or anybody else, you can always reach me at my paper.'

The Reverend Blythe nodded. As Paul got down from the stage and started away between the chairs, the man came forward to the footlights. 'They're all the same,' he said. 'The young people nowadays. They're all searching for an answer. All of them, looking for something . . .'

'Yes, I'm sure.' Paul glanced back at the solitary figure on the flag-decked platform. 'Thanks for your help, vicar,' he said and went on out.

The strip lights were coming on in the news room; for a moment they flickered like theatrical lightning on David Plummer's big Roman face. He sat frowning at Paul, the corners of his mouth drawn down in an expression of doubt and disapproval. 'I admit it's interesting,' he said. 'But we have to be damned careful. After all, you haven't a shred of supporting evidence.'

Paul thought a moment. 'Let's put a dropper in tomorrow's edition,' he said. 'A little news item under my by-line somewhere on the front page. *Religious Sect Links Two Teenage Deaths*. A girl threw herself off my roof and a boy ran his motor-bike off the road. We say nothing

73

about suicide and we don't give the youngsters' names. Nobody can sue us for that. Perhaps there are other parents who've suffered in the same way and are afraid to talk, or people somewhere who know something. If they see a newspaper is writing about it, it might make that little bit of difference.'

Plummer's perfectly round eyes remained sceptical. 'I can hear Merlin's comments now.' He sighed. 'All right, but keep it short – page one's pretty crowded tonight.'

It took Paul ten minutes to write the story. Plummer frowned distrustfully at the piece of copy when he put it on the desk; he was eating a Mars bar and talking to the chief sub on the telephone.

Mrs Clay had said that Rosamond had been to a convent school. Later Nicola had told him that she had been on her way home from school in Wimbledon when she had seen her sister for the last time. It seemed reasonable to suppose that the two places were one and the same. Letting himself into the flat, he went to his study and consulted the telephone directory. There was only one convent in Wimbledon. He dialled the number.

'Convent of the Sisters of Bethlehem,' a voice said.

'Good evening. My name is Paul Marriott. I'm calling about a niece of mine who's at your convent. Nicola Clay.'

'Nicola. Yes?'

'I live abroad and I happen to be passing through London. I went to see Nicola's parents this morning and they told me the dreadful news about Rosamond.'

'Yes, it was a terrible thing,' the voice said. 'Nicola is most upset. We all are.'

'Unfortunately I missed her at Tarrybridge and I have to leave the country again in a day or two. I haven't seen her for a long time and I'd like to take her out to lunch tomorrow.'

There was a little pause. 'I suppose that would be possible. I shall have to speak to the Reverend Mother. If you could come here about noon, she'll be able to see you.'

'Very well. I'll do that.'

'Good-bye, Mr Marriott.'

'Good-bye.' Paul put down the telephone. He hoped that Nicola would play along and that the nuns wouldn't think it necessary to consult her parents. Certainly Nicola had seemed very anxious to tell him something when they had met so briefly outside the house. One way or another he had to know what it was. For a long time he sat staring across the study at the open window. It was dark outside, the hot summer air still and lifeless. He heard the area gate creak as it opened and Mr Kolokowski's limping footsteps cross the yard below. There was the clatter of a dustbin lid, then the footsteps went shuffling away. The gate creaked again. There was silence. He wondered vaguely if Fred were back in the scullery.

The Convent of the Sisters of Bethlehem was a modern brick building standing a little back from a tree-lined road on the south side of Wimbledon Common. Paul rang the bell. The door was opened by a young nun in a pale grey habit, her wimple framing a pretty blue-eyed face. He told her who he was.

'Oh, yes,' the nun said. 'Reverend Mother is expecting you.'

She led him down a long broad corridor towards a flight of stairs; there was a faint smell of wax from the parquet floor. Through a row of steel-framed windows he could see the grounds, a hockey field in the distance. Three girls of fourteen or fifteen, carrying tennis rackets and wearing shorts, came down the stairway. They looked at Paul with interest as they passed. He had dressed carefully for the occasion in a dark suit, white shirt and black tie; he looked eminently respectable, even distinguished. The rest, he thought, was up to Nicola. At the foot of the staircase they turned and followed another corridor at the end of which was a green baize door. The young nun opened the door and knocked on the panel of an inner one.

'Yes, come in.'

The nun held the door open. 'Mr Marriott,' she announced.

Paul entered a large, white-painted office. A window at the far end looked out on sun-lit trees and tennis courts. He was surprised to see an attractive, smartly coiffured woman in a dark suit smiling at him from behind the desk. 'I'm Mother Ashton-Boyd,' she said. 'Won't you please sit down?'

Paul took a chair by the desk. There was a crucifix on the wall behind Mother Ashton-Boyd; otherwise the room was entirely secular and functional in appearance: filing cabinets against one wall, a collection of school photographs above; a vase of carnations on a table by the window and a potted azalea on the desk.

'I've just been writing to Elizabeth,' the nun said. 'We were all deeply shocked at the news about Rosamond. Everyone in the community remembers her with such fondness.'

'Yes, I can believe that,' Paul said. 'She was a very exceptional person.'

'We have to accept it as God's will.' Mother Ashton-Boyd moved the azalea pot a little to one side. 'But how I wish people would realise it's their moral duty to take more care on the roads.'

'I agree entirely.' He had been wondering what the Clays had told the convent.

'I don't remember you coming here to visit the children before,' the nun said. 'But Nicola tells me you're seldom in England.'

'I don't get back as often as I'd like to,' Paul replied. 'I've a business in Hong Kong. It keeps me pretty occupied.'

'Hong Kong?' Mother Ashton-Boyd looked at him in surprise. 'Nicola said something to me about Australia.'

'Yes . . . It's an Australian company. We trade with the

Far East. I divide my time between Hong Kong and Darwin. When I do manage to come to England, it's usually at Christmastime. I'm on my way to New York at the moment. I was anxious to see Nicola before I left.'

'Poor child, she's been very subdued since she got back. But her parents thought it better she should come to school in the usual way. She'll be among her friends and will have something to occupy her. I understand the funeral isn't until late next week.'

'No.'

There was a short silence. The Reverend Mother sat looking at the azaleas in front of her. 'Tell me, how did Elizabeth seem when you saw her?' she asked quietly.

'Oh . . . terribly upset. Utterly lost. I don't think she can quite believe it's happened.'

'And John?' The nun was still staring at the blood-red flowers. From a clock tower somewhere came the chimes of noon.

'Well . . . he's been keeping himself busy. The garden. He does have that.'

'Yes.' The woman turned to him, her calm eyes searching his face. 'Elizabeth and I are very old friends. We were at school together. She must have told you.'

Paul nodded. 'She's mentioned you often.'

The clock stopped chiming. Mother Ashton-Boyd sat back, picked up a pencil and turned it between her fingers. 'Elizabeth Gissing as she was then. She used to write plays for our class to perform and invariably won the poetry prizes. It was from her that Rosamond got her talent.' The disturbingly tranquil eyes rested on Paul again. 'You can't be from her side of the family, surely?'

'No.' Paul smiled. 'The children always called me "Uncle Paul". In fact, I'm related to John's family through marriage. I became "Uncle Paul" to them when they were very young, when I used to see a lot more of them. In the old days, at Maidstone.'

The nun nodded, still watching him. 'I see. I wondered.'

77

There was another silence. The sound of girls' voices and the 'pock-a-pock' of tennis balls came from beyond the window behind Paul. He was beginning to worry. There was no sign of Nicola, nor had there been any indication that she was going to appear. He said, 'Tell me, how is Nicola getting on?'

'Oh, very well. She's a bright child.' The nun gave a faintly wry smile. 'Certainly full of spirit.'

'And her music? How's that progressing?' He remembered the guitar book at Tarrybridge.

'The guitar? Well, she only started last term . . .'

'John told me.'

'Her teacher says she has more enthusiasm than talent. But then enthusiasm has always been her strongest characteristic.'

'Very much so.'

'I think in the end she'll do very well,' Mother Ashton-Boyd said, putting down the pencil. 'With the right guidance. She's a little wild and needs more supervision than most of my girls.' The nun reached out and plucked a dead leaf from the azalea. For what seemed minutes she sat staring at it. 'How long is it in fact since you last saw Nicola?' she asked finally.

'It must be nearly two years,' Paul replied.

Mother Ashton-Boyd dropped the leaf into the azalea pot and turned to him. 'Let me see, would that have been at Maidstone? Or had they already moved to Tarrybridge?'

The question had sounded casual enough. But the nun's eyes had remained fixed upon him, he thought, with a particular watchfulness. He hadn't the faintest idea what the right answer was. Sitting back a moment, he frowned as if in an effort of recollection. 'Fault!' a voice called from beyond the trees; a ripple of laughter followed, liquid-sounding in the stillness.

Just then there was a tap on the door.

'Come in,' the Reverend Mother said.

The door opened rather quickly and Nicola stepped into the room. She was wearing a short, pleated skirt and a white blouse. Giving Mother Ashton-Boyd a respectful nod, she turned and started towards Paul. He had risen to his feet, trying not to show his relief.

'Uncle Paul!' the girl said. 'How lovely to see you again.' She proffered a cheek.

Paul gave her a kiss then stepped back and looked at her. 'Nicola . . . I hardly would have known you. It's been such a long time.'

She looked straight back at him, her wide green eyes oddly expressionless, her smile seeming to fill the whole of her face like a mask.

'I must ask you to have Nicola back at the convent by four o'clock,' Mother Ashton-Boyd said.

'I'll see that she is,' Paul replied.

'Enjoy your afternoon, Nicola.' The nun smiled.

'Yes, Reverend Mother.'

They started across the room. Paul said, 'Good-bye, Mother Ashton-Boyd, and thank you.'

He opened the door and followed Nicola out. They walked side by side down the corridor, both looking straight in front of them and not saying a word, their footsteps loud on the polished parquet. They reached the main door and came out into the hot sunlight.

Still without speaking, they climbed into the car. Not until they had pulled away from the front of the convent did she seem to relax.

'You were wonderful,' he said. 'I wasn't at all sure you'd play along.'

For the first time since they had left the office they looked at one another. 'It's about Rosamond' she said.

'Yes.'

'Why are you so interested?'

'I'm a journalist, a crime reporter. I got involved in the business of your sister's death quite by chance. You were trying to tell me something the other morning. I felt

79

it must be important. I hand to find some way of talking to you.'

She sat looking through the windscreen as they started along the west side of the common. 'Reverend Mother told me my Uncle Paul was coming to take me out. The name meant absolutely nothing to me. I very nearly gave you away. Then she said Paul Marriott and I suddenly realised. I was so surprised . . . She asked me where you came from. I just said – Australia.'

'I know. I managed to field that one. I only hope I don't get you into trouble.'

'It doesn't matter,' she said. 'I want to know the truth.' She turned to him. 'You told Mummy and Daddy it happened where you live. What happened? Please tell me.'

Paul hesitated. 'I live on the top floor of a block of flats,' he said. 'There's an attic above. Apparently she'd been camping there for a while. You can get from the attic – out on to the roof. There's a fire-walk runs just above my study window . . .'

'Oh, dear God.' Nicola turned her head away quickly. 'I'm sorry,' she said after a moment. 'It's all right. Go on.'

Carefully and in detail he told her the story. His conversation with John Aubrey. His visit to the disco pub and his meeting with Gail Canning. How he had found the offices of the Regiment of God and attended their service. Finally his visit to the Tendlers in Islington and his talk with the vicar.

By the time he had finished they were nearly at the bottom of Putney High Street, crawling through the traffic towards the bridge, the pavements crowded with shoppers.

Nicola sat silent for nearly a minute. 'You've done an awful lot in two days,' she said.

'It's my business,' he told her. 'I'm good at it. You understand, I didn't want to drag you into this. But I need your help.'

'I don't mind,' she said in a calm, quiet voice. 'I want to help.'

'You and Rosamond were very close?' he asked.

'No, not really. No one was very close to Rosamond. She was always secretive and unapproachable even when she was small. Mummy and Daddy never understood her. I did a little . . I suppose I was closer to her than anybody.'

'Tell me something else,' Paul said. 'I may be wrong about this. But when I talked to your parents, I had the impression they were frightened.'

'Yes,' she said, looking straight through the windscreen again. 'I think they are, too. I don't know why.' She paused. 'We had a terrible day on Wednesday after the police had been. I wasn't allowed to hear what they said. Then every time I came into the room Mummy and Daddy would stop talking. It was so tense, I can't tell you. That story about the accident. I knew it wasn't true. I wanted so badly to talk to someone. Then you turned up with that notebook of hers . . .' She fell silent a moment then looked at him with a slight frown. 'Are you sure there was only one?'

'Your father asked me the same question,' he said.

'Yes, I heard him. I can't think how he knew. It was one of the last things Rosamond talked to me about. Her notebooks. Three of them. She said they were very important.' Nicola sat a moment staring at her hands. 'Whenever I think of that day, I feel frightened. It's like some horrible dream. I've never had to put it into words before . . .'

'There's no hurry,' he said. 'We'll have a bit of lunch. You can tell me when you feel like it. We've the whole afternoon.'

They crossed Putney Bridge and headed along New King's Road towards Chelsea. He had decided to take her to Antony's, a restaurant he frequented off Beaufort Street. He wasn't sure what Antony would make of

Nicola – he who had seen so many of Paul's girlfriends come and go. But the place was seldom crowded; he would be assured of a quiet table and discreet, unhurried service.

Antony greeted them in the plush little foyer of the restaurant, one wall covered with a photo-mural of the Rue de Rivoli. If he thought that Paul was carrying his taste for very young girls a little far, he gave no sign of it. He was a big, balloon-shaped man of about thirty, prematurely bald, with a round face like an olive and black, liquid eyes.

He led them across the room to a secluded table by the window. Paul was a valued customer and Antony prided himself in the care he took to meet his needs. A demand for a corner table usually meant a new girl. In these cases the service would be leisurely, unobtrusively measured to the mood of the occasion. A wall table as often as not would imply the end of an affair when lunch would be served more briskly, the coffee poured before the pudding had been consumed, so that the unpleasant business need not be unnecessarily prolonged. Then the walk down Beaufort Street and the parting at a taxi in King's Road; a few tears perhaps. 'We'll keep in touch, love.' This was what he always said to his departing girl-friends. 'We'll keep in touch, love.'

'Would you like something to drink?' he asked Nicola as they sat down, Antony attentive at his elbow.

'I'd better not,' she said. 'I haven't a very good head. You wouldn't want to have to deposit me unconscious in Reverend Mother's arms when we got back to the convent.'

Paul glanced up and caught Antony's eye. For the first time in his experience he saw a flicker of astonishment on the man's usually impassive face. 'We'll have a couple of lagers with our food,' he said.

They ordered. For Nicola, a lobster cocktail and grilled Dover sole. For him, mindful of his weight, a tomato salad and Parma ham. Since crossing Putney Bridge they had talked only of generalities: her hatred of convent life, the discipline, the drudgery of O-levels. He had told her a little about his job and one way and another had managed to put her at her ease.

Sitting at the table now, he was able to study her more closely. Her mouth was far too big for her face, so that every expression she made looked exaggerated and somehow comical. At the same time she had an air of self-possession, a disarming directness of manner which made her seem more mature than her years. Watching her, he experienced a certain unease. He had to keep reminding himself that she was only sixteen, hardly older than Naomi, and that this lunch was not at all like the other lunches he had enjoyed in this secluded corner of the restaurant.

Only when she had finished the lobster cocktail did the conversation come back to Rosamond, her eyes clouding, her face becoming serious all at once.

The description she gave of her sister was curiously similar to that which the vicar at the youth club had given him when they had talked about the Tendler boy. Rosamond had been an idealist, very religious and highly artistic. Over-sensitive and diffident about her talent, she had never been able to find a real direction in life. After school, she had stayed at home for nearly a year, writing and taking some interest in local activities – church affairs, charities, the Young Conservatives.

'Was she serious about politics?' Paul asked.

Nicola frowned and took a drink of lager. 'She was serious about her religion, about being a Catholic. And she was violently anti-communist. It used to shock her that the young people she knew found politics such a drag. But then she'd never really been part of the young scene. She had very few friends; she was too shy. She hated parties, she hated crowds. Later, though, she went to live in London, got a job at Harrods, then at a bookshop in

Kensington. She wasn't happy there. Nothing seemed to satisfy her. Then one day Mummy and Daddy got a letter saying she'd joined this religious sect and was going off with them to the country somewhere.'

'No details?'

'No. I saw the letter. It just said a "new religious sect".'

The second course arrived and she started to eat, her face solemn and pensive.

'Weren't your parents worried?' Paul asked.

'They were a little. But then Rosamond had always been a loner. She'd hardly confided in Mummy and Daddy at all since she'd left home. She wrote a couple of times during the next few months, not giving any address, saying she was happier than she'd ever been in her life.' Nicola put down her knife and fork. 'Then last July she wrote to me at school.'

Paul waited. The girl sat thinking for a few moments before she began to speak again. 'The letter arrived just before the end of term. A wild, almost illegible scrawl. She asked me to meet her in London on my way home, in the cafeteria at Waterloo Station. But I was to swear to say nothing to Mummy and Daddy.' She looked helplessly across the table. 'I knew as soon as I saw the letter that something terrible had happened.'

'So you went to the cafeteria,' he prompted.

'Yes. I waited for a while and then she came in. It was such a shock. I hardly recognized her. She looked at least five years older; dirty, thin, undernourished. A real drop-out. I was so shattered, I . . . I didn't think people could change like that. I mean . . . she was Rosamond – and she wasn't Rosamond. As if . . . I don't know . . . everything had been emptied out of her. As if she'd been completely destroyed.'

Nicola sat for a few seconds, picking at her food, a troubled and bewildered expression on her face. Some people got up, laughing, from a near-by table and left the restaurant.

'What happened then?' he asked.

'She sat down and started to talk. She hardly looked at me, as if she only half-realised I was there. She – sort of rambled. A lot of broken, unfinished sentences. I couldn't even hear most of it. Her voice was slurred and very quiet, like – like someone talking in their sleep.'

'Can you remember anything she said?' Paul looked earnestly at Nicola. 'Any little detail. It could be important.'

'Well, she made me promise faithfully – faithfully, faithfully, faithfully – she must have repeated the word twenty times, not to tell Mummy and Daddy I'd seen her. Then something about having failed and being "driven from green fields".' Nicola shook her head briefly. 'It was all so muddled, I couldn't grasp anything properly.'

'You questioned her, though?'

'I tried to. But she wouldn't answer questions. She wasn't being evasive exactly. But my questions seemed to mean nothing to her. She simply ignored them, as if they had no relevance. It's very hard to explain, but . . . she was quite beyond reach, shut up inside herself, cut off – from me, from her surroundings . . . As I said, she was Rosamond and she wasn't Rosamond.'

'What about the doctor? The one John Aubrey talked about?' Paul asked. 'The man in Wimpole Street. Did she say anything about him?'

'She mentioned him once. "The doctor who's my enemy." She wouldn't say why he was an enemy. She said he "knew about the Music Room". Which was perhaps why she was afraid of him.'

'The Music Room . . .' Paul frowned. 'She didn't name the doctor?'

'No. I suppose I should have asked. But I was too upset . . . I begged her to come home, at least to tell me what was wrong so I could help her. But nothing I said was any use. I had the frightening feeling that' — Nicola's wide green eyes met his for a moment — 'that she didn't *know* what had happened to her.'

Paul remained silent for a few seconds. 'What about the notebooks?' he asked.

'She told me there were three notebooks she wanted me to have. She insisted they were very important, though she didn't seem able to say why. She hadn't brought them with her because she was afraid. She said she was being watched all the time, that she was being followed – "by the people from Bloomsbury who had captured God".'

'Do you think she was being followed?' Paul asked after a moment.

'I don't know. I didn't know what to think by then. I was beginning to feel pretty scared myself.' She sat staring at him across the table, her eyes fixed and bright, as if she were on the point of tears. 'It was then she told me she was going to kill herself. She'd send me the notebooks before she died. I was trying to get her to tell me more about the books when she got up suddenly and walked out. I went after her. But by the time I reached the door she'd disappeared in the crowd. I couldn't think what to do . . . I wandered round the station for nearly an hour. Then I took a bus to Victoria and went home.'

'You said nothing to your parents?'

'I should have done, I realise that now. But Rosamond had been so insistent – she'd begged me and begged me. She seemed to have an obsession about it. In any case there was no address, no way of finding her. I kept telling myself it would be all right, that she'd come home. I waited one whole ghastly week – and then it seemed too late to say anything. I tried calling some of her friends in London, but nobody had heard from her in months. So I just went on waiting and praying. Then on Wednesday the police turned up.'

For the rest of lunch Paul questioned her gently and persistently about the conversation in the buffet. But he was able to learn no more. Clearly Nicola had told him everything she knew.

'What are you going to do now?' she asked, sitting beside him in the car as they drove back to the convent.

'It's hard to say. I can't get much further until I know where this training centre is and what goes on there. A house in Berkshire – it doesn't give me much to go on.'

'What about the police?'

He shook his head. 'Unless your parents are prepared to make a formal complaint, they're not likely to do very much. And there's no real evidence at the moment to show that the Regiment of God has done anything criminal. It's no use speculating. In situations like this you just have to keep digging and be very patient.'

They drove in silence round the common. A line of horseback riders cantered by, heraldic shapes against the brown summer grass.

'I wish I knew what she meant about having failed,' Nicola said at last. 'About being "cast out". What could she possibly have done?'

Paul shook his head. 'We're dealing with a bunch of religious and political fanatics, that much is certain. But the sect has existed in America for some years now, and as far as we know nothing like this has happened before. So it has to be something exceptional, something peculiar to this place in Berkshire. That's why I have to find it. Until I do, and until I can get in there, we're only guessing.'

'Get in there?' She looked round at him anxiously.

He smiled. 'I got into your convent, didn't I?'

A moment later he pulled up in front of the building. They got out and walked to the door. He rang the bell. They stood side by side, waiting.

'You will be careful?' she said. 'Anyone who could do a thing like that to Rosamond . . .'

'Don't worry, I'll be all right. I'll get in touch with you the minute there's any news. You know where to reach me if need be.'

She nodded. The young nun in the grey habit opened

the door. Nicola turned and gave him one of her huge, heart-stopping smiles. 'Thank you, Uncle Paul,' she said. 'It was lovely seeing you again.'

Paul kissed her on the cheek and said, 'Goodbye, Nicola.'

He watched her go into the convent. The door closed. Turning, he walked to the car.

As he drove back to town, he had much to think about. The question of the notebooks intrigued him particularly. So there had been three of them. One he had read. The other two had not been among her possessions. If they had been so important, where had Rosamond hidden them? And what clue could they possibly contain to her fate?

The one person you were always certain to see in Earls Court Road on Sunday morning was the old man with the tin whistle. He appeared invariably at the same hour, sidling along the rubbish-strewn pavement opposite the mansion block, his shoulder to the wall, the thin, mournful notes of his whistle filling the deadly Sabbath silence. Paul presumed he was a beggar, though never once in all the years he had lived here had he seen the man collect a penny from anyone. Why he should have chosen this deserted time of the morning to make his slow and furtive progress down the street was a mystery.

Standing at the living-room window, he watched the ragged figure go by, long-shadowed in the morning sunlight. The dismal, tuneless sound of the whistle continued to fill the room as he turned, picked up the telephone and dialled.

'Hello,' a voice said.

'Chris. This is Paul.'

'Paul . . . Good to hear from you. How are you these days?'

'Fine. Look, I've got a little problem for you. Could I drop round for a talk?'

'Sure. Come along.'

'In about ten minutes,' Paul said.

Chris Maitland was his doctor and also an old friend. Usually when Paul visited him it was to have an injury attended to; like the time he had been beaten up by the Triad gangsters in Soho; or on another occasion by a group of thugs hired by a Southall landlord when he had been doing a piece on the exploitation of illegal immigrants. Chris had always maintained that Paul had a charmed life; though Paul was more inclined to attribute his survival to physical fitness and his weekly karate lessons.

The doctor lived in Redcliffe Square, a few minutes' walk from Earls Court Mansions. He was a man of about forty, a hard-working and conscientious GP with a successful private practice. Letting Paul into the flat, he expressed relief at finding him whole and unbloodied.

'What's the problem, then?' he asked, pouring coffee in his study a few minutes later.

'It's a difficult one, Chris.' Paul frowned. 'What do you know about brainwashing, manipulating people's minds? What I'm trying to establish is a technique by which someone could be changed out of all recognition, their personalities completely destroyed.'

Chris looked at him for a moment, a quizzical expression in his clever, slightly down-slanting eyes. 'Trust you to come up with something new in villainy,' he said. 'As a matter of fact, I know next to nothing about it. For obvious reasons there's no literature on the subject. Why are you asking?'

Carefully, Paul recounted the stories of the two dead teenagers. Drawing on Nicola Clay's and John Aubrey's descriptions, he presented as accurate a picture as he could of Rosamond's mental condition, her drug-taking, her inarticulate ramblings, her mortal terror of a place called the Music Room. He finished by adding what little he knew about her life and circumstances before she had disappeared into the ranks of the Regiment of God.

The doctor sat deep in thought for a long time. 'Clinically, I'm afraid I can make very little of it,' he said finally. 'The condition approximates to some form of deep, morbid psychosis associated with rejection and guilt. What I can't understand is how it could have been induced in the minds of two healthy young people during so short a period of time. There are several widely known methods of so-called brainwashing – time disorientation, sleep deprivation and the like – which can, sufficiently prolonged, cause psychotic states. But the results wouldn't necessarily be permanent nor so profoundly destructive as those you've described.' Chris Maitland shook his head slowly. 'I'm afraid I can't think of any explanation. I wouldn't even hazard a guess.'

'Then there's the doctor,' Paul said. 'The one Rosamond Clay referred to as her enemy.'

'Well, I suppose one could envisage such a thing as "black psychiatry",' Chris told him. 'Using psychoanalytical methods to break down a personality rather than put it together. But the process would be very slow and the results no more certain than those of conventional psychiatric treatment.'

Paul got up and walked to the window. A family of white-robed Arabs were sitting on the steps of a house across the square. A child rode by on a tricycle followed by a man reading a Sunday newspaper. 'The extraordinary thing is that, having been given the treatment – presumably at this house in Berkshire – the two youngsters were set free. They were turned loose in London to become – what? Out-patients of the mysterious doctor in Wimpole Street? Surely the sect was taking an incredible risk.'

'It certainly shows a remarkable degree of self-confidence.'

'The kind of self-confidence you'd expect from someone who was a little way round the bend himself.'

There was a brief silence. 'What are you proposing to do about this?' Chris inquired, a faint note of concern in his voice.

Paul turned. 'I'm going to find that Music Room,' he replied. Crossing, he picked up his cup. 'I'll take another coffee off you. Then I have to go and visit a quarantine kennels in Surrey . . .'

He spent an hour touring the kennels, talking to the staff about rabies and being barked at by the inmates. He learned what it cost to keep Fido and Rover in solitary confinement for six months and heard the story of an elderly lady whose chauffeur delivered a quarter of a pound of fillet steak every morning for a vicious-looking, cross-eyed Siamese cat called Ludwig. Ludwig, after only a week in the place, had become totally neurotic and would eat nothing but its own lambswool blankets. There was some doubt as to how long the creature would survive.

In the evening he dined with friends: a fashionable playwright and his wife who lived in Camden Hill. There were three other guests: an equally fashionable dramatic critic, the young actress he happened to be living with at the time and the editor of a women's magazine. As a bachelor and something of a celebrity, Paul was much in demand socially. Dining out was a pastime he enjoyed. For a few hours he was able to forget the green-eyed girl who had lain dead under his study window; the frightened face of her young sister; the preacher's blood-chilling voice at the Kingsway prayer meeting.

The heatwave showed no sign of coming to an end. He passed the following day toiling round ministries and government departments throughout London, asking questions about rabies while inwardly cursing Plummer and Merlin. From a gentle-voiced, grandmotherly woman at the Ministry of Agriculture, he learned about foxes, the principal carriers of rabies in those less favoured lands beyond the Channel; particularly about that new menace, the suburban fox. Foxes, he heard to his surprise, were nightly turning over dustbins in such improbable places as Highgate and Croydon. A heartily cheerful pathologist told him about the filterable virus that was responsible for hydrophobia and proceeded to give him an unnerving description of the symptoms of the disease in man. He discovered that the last recorded case of rabies in the United Kingdom had occurred in 1922. More general statistics revealed that over the past decade human deaths from hydrophobia on the continent of Europe could be counted on the fingers of one badly bitten hand. Finally he visited the Investigation Branch of the Customs and Excise Department who for some reason pretended they knew nothing about the vet in Calais.

He returned to the flat during the late afternoon feeling tired and depressed. He called Plummer and, just to irritate him, delivered a ten-minute lecture on the nocturnal habits of foxes in Croydon.

Just after six o'clock the telephone rang. He took the call in his study.

'Hello, Paul,' a voice said. 'This is Henry.'

'Hello, Henry,' Paul said.

Henry was the City correspondent on another paper, an august journal with a markedly right-wing point of view. He had been at Cambridge with Paul and they had maintained some sort of friendship over the years, though not a particularly close one.

'Haven't seen you in ages, old boy. I just got back from Positano. Too many damned people. You been away?'

'Not yet.'

'Can't think why I asked. Don't you ever let up? You should be sitting on a beach somewhere.'

'I'd be afraid I was missing something.'

'Well, since you are in town, how about a spot of dinner at my club tonight?'

'Yes, fine,' Paul replied.

'Good. About seven-thirty? I'll be waiting for you in the bar.'

Paul put down the telephone, mildly curious. He hadn't heard from Henry in six months; usually the man never called unless he wanted something.

The club was a famous one in Pall Mall, the dark panelled walls hung with paintings of Grenadiers charging foreign-looking soldiers and British men-o'-war firing broadsides at foreign-looking ports.

'How's the fascist press?' Paul asked as he greeted Henry in the bar.

'Selling more papers than you blush-pink liberals.'

On the rare occasions that they met, they always indulged in this kind of banter. It gave the illusion of warmth to a friendship which had long gone cold and which each maintained partly out of self-interest and partly out of habit. Henry was a short, solidly built man with a florid punch-like face that would have been jovial but for a pair of grey, still and curiously watchful eyes. One of the most highly regarded financial editors in Fleet Street, famous for the accuracy and penetration of his commentaries, he was rumoured to be something of an *eminence grise* in the City. An urbane, shadowy and self-effacing figure, he knew everybody and went everywhere, including among his close friends a number of astonishingly influential people. Paul had always admired the man, though of late he had been unable to decide whether he still liked him.

Henry ordered drinks and they sat talking shop for a while. Then Paul noticed a man coming slowly and ponderously towards their table: an unruly head of white hair above a rather coarse and sullen face; a dark and ill-fitting suit of some heavy material quite inappropriate to the season; a rounded, old-fashioned collar and a regimental tie.

'Claude . . .' Henry said, rising and smiling at the

93

newcomer. He turned to Paul. 'This is Claude Stapleton . . . Paul Marriott.'

'How do you do?' Claude Stapleton said in a curiously harsh and off-key voice. Sitting down, he told Henry he would have a tomato juice.

From the distance, Paul had put the man's age at around forty-five. Looking at him across the table now, he realised that he was much younger, probably still in his thirties. The slow and somewhat stooping walk, the outmoded cut of his clothes and the white hair had misled him. Claude, it appeared, was a merchant banker and the conversation soon turned to matters of commerce and finance. Paul sipped his drink and listened. He was beginning to wonder why he had been brought along. Henry certainly wasn't a man who wasted his time on casual socialising.

Fifteen minutes later the three of them finished their drinks and went upstairs to the dining room.

The talk was again principally about City affairs, Claude delivering endless dissertations on the condition of the stock market which somehow sounded as if they had been learned by heart. As before, Paul was content to listen and wait. Claude Stapleton was an excruciating bore even by Henry's standards; also a bit of an oddity. Everything about the man seemed to be borrowed: his opinions, his clothes, his goose-like voice, even the added years he appeared to carry. If Henry were aware of Paul's puzzlement and boredom, he gave no sign of it. Smoothly affable and polite, he drew Paul into the conversation as often as seemed necessary, otherwise listening with apparent interest to the honking second-hand inanities of his other guest.

Towards the end of dinner Claude suggested they 'pop over to Belgrave Square to have a night-cap with Daddy'. Paul, by now convinced that something was being set up for his benefit, did not demur.

They travelled by taxi. The house was on the Chapel

Street side of the square. Climbing the steps, they waited while Claude unlocked the front door.

'Daddy', Paul had already learned, was General Sir Ian Stapleton: a retired soldier who had made a name for himself as a highly sophisticated counter-insurgency fighter in places like Malaya, Aden and Oman during the 1950s and early 1960s. Since then he had dabbled in politics and had gained some notoriety for his outspoken criticisms of the welfare state, socialism, the permissive society and the degeneracy of modern youth.

'I think they must be in the garden,' Claude said in his loud, uncontrolled voice as he led them down the hallway to a glass door at the back of the house.

They passed through the door and descended a short flight of steps to a paved garden. Two men and a woman were seated at a wrought-iron table under a lime tree lit by a single amber-coloured lamp. Claude introduced Paul to the group: Lady Diana Beresford, General Stapleton and Colonel Ferris.

'Hello, Punch.' The colonel greeted Henry warmly after he had shaken hands with Paul. 'How's the Stock Exchange? Don't often get a chance to pick your brains. Come and sit beside me.'

More chairs were produced while Claude served coffee and Delamain brandy from another table. Diana Beresford, Paul knew, was the daughter of the proprietor of Henry's paper; a widow, a socialite and a famous race-horse owner. She was a tall, statuesque woman with the kind of classical beauty he had never particularly admired. Her age might have been around forty, her figure still youthful-looking in a white halter-necked dress. Stirring his coffee, Paul turned his attention to the general. He had seen photographs of him in the press, but somehow these hadn't caught the personality of the man. There was nothing in the least military about his appearance. His face, with its small fine features, was rather that of a scholar: gentle, self-disciplined and withdrawn. At a

95

glance, he might have been mistaken for a senior member of the clergy. Colonel Ferris, several years older than the general, was a shrunken-looking man well below middle height with sandy-grey hair parted and brushed close to his head. He had a reputation for being something of an eccentric, though his appearance betrayed no suggestion of this. There was a kind of immaturity about his round, undistinguished face which, but for the bristle of a moustache, resembled that of a tired schoolboy. His name was as much a household word as the general's. A hero of the Second World War, he had drawn attention to himself in later years as a violent reactionary, the extreme nature of whose views had at times caused embarrassment even to his closest friends. He was a leading member, Paul now recalled, of a shadowy right-wing pressure group called the Excalibur Society – a society which advocated such things as greater expenditure on national defence as opposed to social welfare, a stronger line against militant unionism and the formation of an armed mobile police force to combat terrorism and social disorder.

These then were Paul's companions under the lime tree. That he had been invited here for some ulterior and as yet unrevealed purpose he did not for a moment doubt. At the same time, the atmosphere around the table could hardly have been more civilised and relaxed. He was being made to feel as if it were the most natural thing in the world that he should have dropped in by chance with a fellow journalist for a late night drink. The conversation, to begin with, was on the most neutral level, polite and rather banal: the heatwave, the influx of tourists into London, some problems Lady Beresford was having with her string of racehorses in the country.

Then, in a seemingly casual way, the talk turned to the subject of the press. Henry had something to say about the current economic plight of the newspaper industry, adding his customarily well-informed views about a recent takeover of one of the national dailies. The group

96

listened with interest and respect. Henry was nothing if not a good talker.

'Afraid I don't read your paper, Mr Marriott.' Colonel Ferris turned to Paul finally. 'But I'm told you're one of these investigative journalists. Very fashionable thing to be nowadays. All the rage in America, I believe.'

'Well, it's rather easier for the Americans,' Paul replied. 'Their approach to news reporting is a good deal less inhibited than our own.'

'On the other hand, I'm one of your regular fans,' Lady Beresford said to him. 'I read all your crime reports. I find them absolutely fascinating.'

'Thank you. I'm very flattered,' Paul said, though he didn't believe her. If Diana Beresford read any newspaper, it would certainly be her father's; that is, when she wasn't engrossed in *Horse and Hound* and *Country Life*. He only wondered why she should profess such an interest in his work.

Smiling, she looked briefly at General Stapleton. 'Mr Marriott is the frustrated Hercules of Fleet Street, for ever wanting to cleanse the Augean stable of modern society.'

'No, merely pry into a few dark corners,' Paul said.

'And disturb the spiders?' The smile, the friendly dark eyes were on him now.

'Only the dangerous ones,' he told her.

'And what tarantula are you hunting at the moment? Are we allowed to know?'

'A particularly deadly one. But I'm afraid I have to keep it under wraps.'

'You couldn't even tell us a little?'

Paul shook his head. 'Investigative reporting is a high-risk occupation in this country, Lady Beresford. You've no idea how cautious one has to be.'

'I'd never have thought of you as being cautious,' the woman said. 'What a pity. I was looking forward to some delicious piece of scandal.'

97

'What's your view, Punch?' General Stapleton looked across the table at Henry. 'Do you think British news reporters are unduly restricted about what they're allowed to write?'

Henry appeared to consider the question carefully. 'There's some truth in what Paul Marriott says. Journalists in this country are required to work under a system of prior restraints which the Americans would regard as an infringement of their constitutional rights. Our libel laws, contempt of court rules, the principle of confidence, D notices and the rest – a formidable array of fences, I agree. But for the most part I believe they serve the public good.' He paused and his disturbingly still, grey eyes rested on Paul for a moment. 'What we have to remember above all, I think, is that people who work for the mass media – particularly for the newspapers – carry a very heavy burden of responsibility.'

'Responsibility. Yes.' General Stapleton picked up his glass and took a sip of brandy. 'Responsibility.' He seemed to savour the word with the Delamain, at the same time smiling in a thoughtful way at Paul. 'Now, I do read your newspaper from time to time. I think it's damned good. But – just to take one example – those articles you wrote about the Robbery Squad. The practices of the officers you named were indefensible, I agree. I'd be the first to condemn them. But do you really think the facts should have been printed? Goodness knows, the forces of law and order need all the support they can get in these difficult times. You honestly think it right?'

'Yes, I do,' Paul said quietly, aware that they were all watching him. 'I mean, what kind of paper is it that only prints the good news? It's the public who pay for the police force, after all. Just as they elect their rulers. In my view, government agencies have no more right to cover up their sins and excesses than have private individuals. Less right, in fact.'

98

There was a short silence. The general was still smiling. 'You were drawing a comparison with America just now,' he said in a gentle, almost benign voice. Leaning forward, his slim and erect figure shadowy in the lamplight, he moved his glass and placed his folded hands on the table. 'The Americans are a rich and powerful people. Unlike us, they're still a true democracy. They have a sense of patriotism, a sense of unity and a respect for religion and law which we sadly – and dangerously – lack. They're secure enough to be able to wash their dirty linen in public. They can threaten to impeach their President, blow their own intelligence agency, publicise their scandals in open committees and in the press without fear of unleashing catastrophically divisive forces throughout their society. We, on the other hand, are a divided and threatened people, fatally cut off from all the traditions, moral values and social conventions of the past – it might be said, face to face with the enemy in the front line. Or more truly, grappling with him inside our very walls. Far from practising too much restraint within our mass media, it seems to me we're practising too little. To change my metaphor' — he reached out, resting a hand briefly on Diana Beresford's arm — 'and come to the end of a rather long speech. . . . Since we're foundering, is this really the time to rock the boat?'

'Very well put,' Colonel Ferris said. 'The front line. Exactly.' He looked round at Paul. 'We should be beating the drum, not putting our foot through it – that's my opinion. All it does is give encouragement to the damned communists. Not that they need much.'

'I know this is an old argument.' Paul spoke slowly and carefully. 'But isn't there an almost equal danger? That in overreacting to the communist threat, we could lose the very liberties we're so anxious to defend. Surely the McCarthy era in America was a very good example. . . .'

'There's no similarity at all between the McCarthy business and what's going on in Britain now,' the general

99

said. 'I've spent most of my life fighting the communists in various corners of the globe. I've no illusions about them. And you should have none either. You may think we're a lot of old-fashioned scaremongers, but I wonder if it isn't you who's out of date. The communists mean to dominate the world, they mean to destroy our society. Let's have no doubt about that. I'm in possession of much information that would startle you if I were allowed to reveal it.' He paused; a gentle breeze rustled the leaves of the lime tree above his head. 'I was in Northern Ireland only a little while ago. You can see there what happens when people try to settle political issues in the streets. Though mind you, we're learning a great deal in Ulster that might be useful to us one of these days. Watching events there is perhaps a bit like watching a rehearsal for the future. Nobody wants it to happen, but we're sliding inevitably towards it – towards a confrontation with the extreme left; a massive economic and social breakdown when I believe people will have to choose between communism and some kind of reponsible authoritarian government.' He finished his coffee and sat for a few seconds gazing at his empty cup. 'But to come back to what we were first talking about – the duty of journalists. I think in these times of national crisis they should be aware of the moral burden they're carrying. They're performing a serious duty to the nation and must be quite clear in their minds whose side they're on.'

'Ian,' Lady Beresford said, 'aren't we getting a little gloomy? I shan't sleep tonight. You've castigated poor Mr Marriott quite enough. What ever will he think of us? I've no idea how this conversation started in the first place.'

'With tarantulas,' Paul said.

'We have our spiders, you have yours.' She gave him another smile. 'We shall see one of these days which are the more deadly. Claude, you can give me another very small brandy.'

Claude got up and went to pour the drink.

'What about this horse of yours, Diana?' Colonel Ferris said. 'Should I back it on Saturday?'

'No, I wouldn't if I were you,' she told him. 'My stables, if not quite Augean, have been a little disorganised this year.'

The conversation continued for another quarter of an hour or so. Then Diana Beresford announced that she must go home and the party broke up.

They exchanged good nights in the hall and Paul went down the steps with Henry and Diana Beresford. Here Henry left them, saying he was going to walk to his flat in Eaton Square. Lady Beresford, who had a town house in The Boltons, offered to drive Paul part of the way home. Crossing the pavement, he climbed into the passenger seat of her white Daimler Sovereign.

It was after midnight and there was little traffic as they headed along Knightsbridge and Brompton Road.

'I'm afraid you can't have enjoyed your evening very much,' she said finally. 'I feel quite guilty about it. Those three men gave you a pretty bad time.'

'I'm used to being knocked about,' he told her.

She turned her head and looked at him. 'So I see. But it shouldn't include being bullied by my friends, especially when they'd never set eyes on you before.'

'I'm sure they meant it for the best,' Paul said. 'They struck me as being very sincere.'

Diana Beresford gave a little sigh. 'We all worry about England and what is to become of her. And then Ian Stapleton is extraordinarily well informed. I'm not supposed to know, but he's still very much *involved* if you follow me. Things to do with national security.'

'And Colonel Ferris?'

'Also, I believe. . . . But there – perhaps I'm saying more than I should.' She looked round at him again, a warm smile on her lips. 'I thought you held your own very well. I'm sure Ian respected you for it.'

How nice, he reflected sourly, to have Ian's respect. It had almost made his day. 'I presume you share his views?' he said. 'That before long all the decent chaps will be manning the barricades.'

'No more politics.' She gave a soft, pleasant laugh. 'Actually I find the subject rather boring. When it doesn't frighten me. There are more entertaining things to do than sit around predicting one's own doom.'

He supposed she must mean keeping horses. It was the one topic on which he was incapable of conducting a conversation. They continued in silence for a while, taking the turn into Old Brompton Road at just over fifty. She drove, as he imagined she did everything else, with skill, assurance and scant regard for the rules that governed the lives of ordinary mortals.

As they approached The Boltons she didn't slow down but surprised him by swinging round the corner and speeding on down the street.

'You'll have a brandy with me,' she said. 'After all you've been subjected to, I'm determined your evening shall end pleasurably.'

He said nothing. She stopped the car. He got out. His mind filled with speculations, he followed her across the pavement to the house.

They went up to the drawing room on the first floor. The curtains were already drawn, white brocade against pale yellow silk wall coverings. A silver-framed photograph of Diana Beresford sitting on a horse; another of a man, presumably her late husband, leading a winner at some race meeting. A row of invitation cards on the mantelpiece; a landscape painting up above which he felt sure must be a Constable. The woman poured two glasses of brandy and he took one from her.

'Come and sit beside me,' she said.

They crossed the room and sat together on the sofa. She sat very close to him. He noticed that her eyes weren't black as he had thought but very dark brown. Her bare shoulders and her throat shone moist in the light of the single lamp that illuminated the room. It occurred to him that he had never made love to a woman of his own age. He found the prospect more exciting than he would have anticipated.

She took a sip of brandy. 'To the barricades,' she said.

He shook his head. 'Barricades are for romantics.'

'I was wrong about your Herculean ambitions, then?'

'Quite wrong. I've no illusions about the world I live in. I can't change it and I don't wish to try.'

'The spiders, though?'

'People want to read about the spiders. I write about them rather well. It helps to sell my newspaper.'

'I only half-believe you.' She reached out and ran the tip of her finger along the scar on his cheek. 'Tell me how you got that.'

He told her.

She sat back and drank a little more brandy. 'But you won't tell me what this story is you're writing now. The latest scandal that's going to shock the country.'

'I'm afraid not,' he said.

'Why?'

'Because you might tell somebody else. The word would get around and the story would be blown before my paper could print it.'

'Whom would I tell? Ian Stapleton?'

'I thought we agreed not to talk politics. You said there was to be a pleasurable end to the evening.'

'I hadn't forgotten.' She put her glass down.

He thought, in about thirty seconds she'll get up and leave the room. A few minutes later she'll come back wearing a chiffon négligée and smelling faintly of Chanel Number Five.

After about thirty seconds she got up and left the room. A few minutes later she came back wearing nothing at all and smelling faintly of Schiaparelli's Shocking. He was on his feet. She came straight across the room and put her arms around him. He kissed her. There was nothing feigned, he felt sure, about her response, the quick eagerness of her arousal. She took him by the hand and led him to the door, along a landing and up a flight of stairs to her bedroom. He hoped she would be better in bed than she had been at playing Mata Hari on the sofa.

He wasn't disappointed. Diana Beresford's repertoire was at least as comprehensive as his own. He had to admit that she was more entertaining and more demanding than many of the twenty-year-olds he had taken to Earls Court Mansions. It was an experience, he realised, that he would be happy to repeat. Only once again did she ask him about his present newspaper assignment. He retaliated by telling her about the Croydon foxes. After that she gave up and they simply enjoyed themselves. Nothing marred his pleasure but an occasional thought of the four men under the lime tree.

At five he got out of bed and put on his clothes. She rose also and walked with him, naked, down the two flights of stairs to the hall. Opening the front door, she said, 'I'm giving a little luncheon party in the country on Friday. There'll be some people from the newspaper world who it might be interesting and useful for you to meet. Please tell me you'll come.'

'I'd love to,' he said.

She gave him the address and instructions how to get there. He kissed her, said good night and went out into the warm darkness.

The door closed softly behind him as he descended the steps. Slowly he made his way up the street past the elegant white-fronted houses, past the dim shape of St Mary's church on its tree-covered island.

First a lecture on the responsibilities of the press; then Lady Diana's bed and the offer of patronage. He couldn't believe that the evening's encounter had been accidental. But what could have prompted it? Surely not the brief news story about Rosamond Clay and Jack Tendler in the paper last week. He frowned to himself. The dingy office in Coptic Street and the two dead youngsters. Try as he would, he couldn't relate these with the shadowy men of power sitting under the tree in the Belgrave Square garden.

The paper's political correspondent, Duncan Keswick, had his office on the floor above the news room. He was a small, precise man of some fifty years with a high bald head and a dryly cynical manner.

'The Excalibur Society?' he said, looking across the desk at Paul. 'I know a great deal about them. Why are you interested?'

'I'll tell you in a moment,' Paul replied. 'But I was invited to a little soirée last night at the home of General Stapleton in Belgrave Square. Colonel Ferris was one of the guests.'

'Oh, Ferris. Yes. I don't suppose I need tell you about him.'

'Not really. He's been involved in all manner of wildcat schemes in his time, like raising a private army to go out pranging the proletariat when the revolution came – the "Loyalist Brigade" or some such thing.'

Duncan Keswick nodded. 'He and Stapleton were founder members of the Excalibur Society. It started out as a small right-wing group composed principally of retired soldiers, mainly supporters of the defence lobby, the "Keep Britain Great" faction'. Keswick opened a tartan tobacco pouch and began slowly and methodically filling his pipe. 'But since then it's become a vastly more elaborate and more powerful organisation. I imagine it's rather outgrown people like Stapleton and Ferris. We tried to do a big piece on Excalibur at one time, but for a number of reasons we had to drop the idea.' He put down the pouch and looked at Paul seriously for a moment. 'I should warn you this is an extremely sensitive subject. From the political and security point of view, you could say it was near to being dynamite.'

Paul sighed. 'All right, tell me the worst,' he said.

Keswick started searching for a box of matches among the litter of papers on his desk. 'The Excalibur Society has several highly placed politicians on its council, as well as captains of industry from some of the plushier boardrooms. The address of its London office is a closely guarded secret and no one seems to know where its funds come from. Its aims, which it pursues through lobbying and propaganda, are mainly to swing Tory policy to the extreme right and to awaken people to the dangers of Soviet infiltration of British institutions and industry. But that's not the whole story by any means.' Keswick was going through his pockets now, looking for the matches. 'Excalibur is in fact only one part of a closely knit web of organisations. Among these is the Acropolis Publishing Company which produces books in a series called "Contemporary Viewpoint". I don't know if you've heard of them.'

'Acropolis.' Paul thought a moment. 'The name rings a bell.'

'Soft-sell right-wing propaganda. Their books are distributed in Britain, America and many of the Third World countries.' Keswick gave up searching his pockets for the matches and sat a moment looking disappointedly at his unlit pipe. 'Acropolis' parent company is a concern called West Coast Enterprises in Washington. Try to telephone them and you'll find it's an answering service. Acropolis is in fact wholly financed by the CIA.'

'Oh, Christ.' Paul got up and walked to the window. The temperature in the room must have been over eighty. He felt a trickle of sweat run down the back of his collar.

'Closely linked with Acropolis', Keswick went on, 'is a third organisation called the Confederation for International Studies. This was set up a year or so ago with the blessing of the British intelligence services and some very highly placed people in the Establishment. Its purpose is to collect and analyse information about subversion and terrorism throughout the world. It issues confidential

106

pamphlets, mainly on counter-insurgency tactics, and arranges lectures. Among its clients are police training colleges, the Military College of Science, the Army Staff College, the Special Air Service, the Chemical Warfare Research Centre at Porton Down and the South African and Rhodesian security services. Its chief subscriber is the US Association for Political Studies.' Duncan Keswick was searching for his matches again. 'This time an answering service in Delaware.'

For a few seconds Paul stood gazing out of the window. A pigeon landed on the ledge outside; feathers ruffled, it stared at him through a baleful, half-closed eye. It looked sick. He said, 'All this started because I was looking into the affairs of a religious sect called the Regiment of God.'

'Oh, yes,' Keswick said. 'I saw your story on the front page last week. I was wondering.'

Briefly Paul told him what he knew about General Anderton and the Fifth Church of the Eternal Spirit in Coptic Street. He went on to describe his evening in Belgrave Square. 'It seems to me there has to be some kind of connection between General Anderton's church and the Excalibur Society,' he finished.

The political correspondent sat back, holding his unlit pipe at arm's length. 'I think it's very unlikely,' he said. 'From what you've told me, the Coptic Street sect sounds far too insignificant to interest people like Stapleton and Ferris.'

'But they could have met General Anderton at some time.'

'Yes.' Keswick sat forward slowly, running a hand over his bald head. 'It's all a bit tenuous though, isn't it?'

'Perhaps.' Paul came away from the window. All at once he stopped and said, 'Acropolis – just a minute. Wasn't that the company run by a man called Gerald McDermot who was blown up in his car last Tuesday?'

'Why, yes. The Provos have finally claimed credit for the murder. As it happens, McDermot was one of the

107

leading brains in the Confederation for International Studies.'

'He was?' Paul stood looking down at the carpet for a moment. Then he nodded and started for the door.

'Paul . . .'

The other turned.

'Leave it alone,' Keswick said. 'If Merlin knew you were raking around in that hornets' nest, he'd have your guts.'

Paul only smiled and opened the door. 'Thanks for the briefing,' he said.

An hour later he was pacing the living room of his flat. Duncan Keswick had suggested that General Stapleton and Colonel Ferris represented the more extreme views of the Excalibur Society. The Colonel's history, certainly, would put him as near as mattered to the lunatic fringe of political thought. What still puzzled him was why the two men had been so extraordinarily inept. By inviting him to Belgrave Square they had to all intents and purposes disclosed their interest in the Regiment of God. Either they were being very stupid or they were more than a little desperate, anxious to silence him by any means, however hurriedly and clumsily contrived. But what were they so afraid of? And why the urgency? He was still pondering the problem when he heard a ring at the doorbell.

Going along the hall, he opened the door. The last thing he had expected was a visit from the police. And the last member of the force he wanted to see standing on his doorstep was Chief Inspector Trahearne of the Serious Crimes Squad. Trahearne looked very serious indeed; his broad, heavily jowled face was a bit like Leonid Brezhnev's without any of the humour. Standing beside him was a young fair-haired detective, as mean-looking as an underfed cat.

'Good afternoon, Mr Marriott,' Trahearne said. 'May we have a word with you?'

'Certainly.' Paul stepped aside. 'Come in.'

The two men entered the hall. Trahearne took off his hat and placed it on a table beside him.

'This way,' Paul said and led them to the living room. He had met Trahearne only once before, with Chief Superintendent Meedon at the Yard when they had played the tapes for the Robbery Squad corruption story. It hadn't been a very pleasant occasion. He didn't need to remind himself that Meedon, once in charge of the Robbery Squad, was now Commander, Serious Crimes, and Trahearne's immediate superior. Moreover Trahearne had the reputation of being one of the toughest and shrewdest officers in the Metropolitan Police. Whatever he had come here for, it wasn't to make a social call.

The three men came into the living room and sat down. Trahearne seemed to be in no hurry. Running a large finger round the inside of his collar, he sat staring absently out of the window for a few seconds.

Finally he said, 'We wanted to talk to you about a young woman called Rosamond Clay, Mr Marriott.'

'Oh – the suicide.'

'The alleged suicide, sir.' The detective sat back in his chair. 'We wondered how well you knew the young lady?'

'Knew her? I didn't know her. You must have seen the statement I made to the police when they came here.'

'Yes, we read your statement,' Trahearne said in a flat voice, his big, Siberian face turned squarely to Paul.

There was a brief silence. Whatever Paul had expected from Trahearne, it certainly hadn't been this. 'So you read the statement. That's what happened,' he said.

The Chief Inspector frowned; his expression seemed to be one of genuine puzzlement. 'You're quite sure Miss Clay wasn't living with you in this flat?' he asked.

Paul got suddenly to his feet. 'Look, for Christ's sake – the first time I saw Rosamond Clay was when she went hurtling past my study window at ten o'clock last Wednesday morning.'

109

'Went hurtling past your window.' The phrase seemed to appeal to Trahearne. He sat a moment as if he were meditating on it. Then he said, 'So you dialled 999 and a car came round from Kensington police station.'

'Yes. I talked to a sergeant and a constable.'

'Sergeant Ives, sir.'

'I showed them the body. Later we met up in the attic here where the girl had been living. She and a young man. The police saw the parapet from which she jumped, also her sleeping bag and a suitcase which presumably they took away.'

'Yes, I had a look at her things,' Trahearne told him.

'All right then. Suppose you explain what all this is about.'

The detective nodded. 'We've received an inquiry about Miss Clay,' he said. 'The inquirer had been trying to trace her. He seemed to think she'd been living at Earls Court Mansions and mentioned the name of Marriott.'

'If someone thought Rosamond Clay was living here, why didn't they come and ask me?' Paul demanded.

'The person said he'd telephoned you several times but had been unable to get a satisfactory reply.'

'The person? What person?'

'You maintain you've received no such telephone calls?'

'Of course I haven't,' Paul said.

'The man's name is George Cathcart,' Trahearne told him. 'He claims to be a friend of Miss Clay's. He said he'd met her a couple of weeks ago at a discotheque in King's Road.'

'He's a bloody liar,' Paul said. 'Rosamond Clay was living in the attic upstairs with a young man called John Aubrey. Aubrey turned up on Wednesday evening to collect his bag – a bag which Sergeant Ives saw. I stopped Aubrey on the stairs and we had a long talk. He'd been with the Clay girl for the better part of a week. He said nothing about her having any friends. In fact it's highly

110

unlikely she would have had any.'

'Oh? Why do you say that, sir?'

'She was out of her mind, half-crazy. She belonged to a religious sect called the Regiment of God. I believe she'd been got at in some way – brainwashed, terrorised. If you want to know why she's dead they're the people you should be talking to, not me.'

'We know the young woman belonged to a religious group,' Trahearne said imperturbably. 'But no one has said anything to us about her mental condition.'

'Then George Cathcart has to be lying,' Paul replied. 'Perhaps he's a member of the Regiment of God.'

'I've no idea, sir. But tell me, where is Mr Aubrey now?'

'I don't know. I've reason to believe he's a drug addict. He said he was going to find a new pad in Shepherd's Bush.'

'A drug addict of no fixed address,' Trahearne said softly. He sat a moment staring at his hands. Then he got up slowly from the chair. 'Could we have a look at your study, Mr Marriott? The window.'

'Yes, come along.' Paul led them to the door.

They crossed the passage and came into the study. The window was still open. The young detective stood just inside the doorway and Trahearne walked to the middle of the room. 'Let's see,' he said. 'You were sitting at your desk.'

'Sitting at my desk when I heard a scream. I looked up and saw the body go past the window.'

'The body hurtle past the window.' The Chief Inspector moved across the room, leaned on the sill and looked down into the area. After a moment he twisted his body and looked up at the parapet directly above. 'And there were no other witnesses at all?'

'As Sergeant Ives must have told you.'

Trahearne turned from the window. The young detective took out a handkerchief and dabbed his forehead.

111

After a long moment Trahearne said, 'I spoke to Mr and Mrs Clay this morning. They told me you'd called on them on Thursday and returned a notebook belonging to their daughter. A notebook containing poems.'

'That's perfectly correct,' Paul said.

Trahearne stood looking at him, a deep frown on his heavy, commissar's face. 'Where did you get the notebook, sir?'

Paul hestitated. The cat-faced detective folded his arms and shifted his weight from one foot to the other. 'I went up to the attic ahead of Sergeant Ives and the constable,' Paul said finally. 'I saw the book lying on the girl's sleeping bag and picked it up. What I read interested me. I didn't think the book would be of any value to the police, so I decided to keep it.'

'You decided to keep it.' Trahearne made a little grimace. Coming slowly up the room, he put his hands on the desk. 'You don't think it a little odd that you should have purloined a notebook belonging to a young woman you claim you'd never seen before – a book which might well have been evidence in what was clearly a police matter? And having done that, you go to all the trouble of finding out her address and driving down to Sussex to visit her parents.'

'I was curious,' Paul replied. 'As I said, the verses interested me. There was something about the whole business that made me want to know more. You forget, I'm a newspaperman.'

Trahearne gave him a long, hard, unfriendly look. 'No, I hadn't forgotten that, sir.' He turned to the window again. 'When you spoke to Mr and Mrs Clay, you made some point of asking whether there were any other notebooks, writings belonging to their daughter, and where these might be found.' With a quick movement of his head, he looked back at Paul.

'Yes, I did. I thought there might be some possibility of collecting her works and getting them published.'

112

'Getting them published.' Trahearne stood staring at him for a moment. Then he took a few paces towards the door and paused. 'May I ask if you've made any effort to find more of the books, sir? Talked to her friends, other relatives, anything like that?'

'No,' Paul answered, thinking of Nicola.

'Then you've nothing to add to what you've already said?'

'Nothing,' Paul replied.

'Very well, sir. I think that'll be all for the moment.'

Trahearne and the fair young man left the room. Paul followed them to the front door. The Chief Inspector picked up his hat and said, 'You weren't planning to leave London by any chance? Take a holiday or anything like that?'

'No, I shall be here,' Paul told him. And he opened the door.

The two men went out. 'Good day, Mr Marriott, and thank you,' Trahearne said.

Paul closed the door and walked back to the living room. The turn of events had been so unexpected that he still wasn't thinking very clearly. Behind it all he felt sure he could discern the vengeful figure of Commander Meedon. But who had produced the mysterious witness George Cathcart? He thought again of the men under the lime tree. Duncan Keswick had told him that the Excalibur Society, through the Confederation for International Studies, maintained close links with the police. Then there were the notebooks. Why had Trahearne laid so much emphasis on them? For several minutes he stood staring uneasily into the fireplace. It was beginning to seem that this time he had disturbed a whole nest of spiders.

Part Two
THE MUSIC ROOM

If you want to learn something about God, the most likely person to ask is the Devil.

Acting on this principle, Paul visited a public house in Notting Hill Gate next day. The Volunteer stood on the corner of a street that was at once garish and derelict-looking; a house-front here and there painted purple, orange and brilliant yellow. The sound of a calypso band came loud through an open window.

He pushed his way into the public bar, for it was here he hoped to find Harry Leavis. Most of the lunch-hour customers were West Indians; but sure enough, seated in his usual corner by the window, was the man he sought – Harry, with his government-surplus gas-mask haversack open in front of him, the table littered with papers as he scribbled away. Harry was an old-fashioned hard-line orthodox Marxist, a self-made intellectual who wrote pamphlets for left-wing militant organisations and busied himself devotedly in various ways, some of them rather obscure, to the furtherance of the world communist revolution. He was an elderly, scruffy man, a bachelor, a fanatic and a born conspirator. With his elaborate network of contacts throughout the political underworld, he had been useful to Paul on more than one occasion. There was indeed little he didn't know about the subversive organisations operating in and around London, were they Marxist, Trotskyist, Maoist, anarchist or separatist.

'Harry, good morning,' Paul said, coming up to the table.

'Paul . . .' Harry looked up, pushing a pair of greasy spectacles on to his forehead. He had small sharp eyes, his face gnarled and white like a guttered candle. 'Good to see you, my lad. How are things?'

'Active,' Paul replied. 'I need your help. Can you spare me a few minutes?'

'Of course, of course,' Leavis said in his thin, reedy and surprisingly cultured voice. 'Always glad to help a fellow writer.'

'I'll get you a drink.' Paul picked up an empty glass from the table.

'Good of you, good of you.' The old man started gathering up his papers and stuffing them into the khaki haversack.

Paul crossed to the bar. Harry Leavis the revolutionary was also a drinker; he wrote his polemics on copious draughts of brandy and water; for this reason a few fivers slipped into his hand were always welcome.

Returning with the brandy and a glass of lager, Paul sat down.

'Is it Carlos Illich Ramirez?' Harry said. 'He's been reported happy and well in Tripoli.'

'I'm not interested in Carlos,' Paul told him. 'This is something quite else.' He took a sip of beer. 'Shall we say twenty-five quid for a start?'

Harry gave a little shrug, indicating agreement. Paul produced the money and, swift as a conjurer, Leavis transferred it to his breast pocket. 'You look to me like a worried man,' he said.

'I am worried.' Paul put his elbows on the table. 'I'm being pushed. I need some information and I need it very urgently. Did you ever hear of an American called General Lee Anderton, founded a crackpot religious group called the Regiment of God?'

'Never in my life,' Harry replied.

'The Excalibur Society, then?'

The other raised his eyebrows; they were jet black unlike his hair which was yellowy white in colour. 'Ah now, there you're talking,' he said. 'A very high-class outfit indeed. Wog-bashing soldiers, fascist literary gents

118

and last-ditch boardroom johnnies trying to rally the Establishment against the workers and the unions. A lot of talk about private armies, squads of para-military strike breakers and the rest. Shades of the old *Sturmabteilung*.' He took a pull at his brandy and water. 'They're not to be underestimated, Paul. The right-wing vigilante movements are getting to be quite fashionable nowadays. They're all over South America and we've already seen a bit of it in Spain and Italy.'

'The Excalibur Society, the Confederation for International Studies and a publishing company called Acropolis.'

'Strewth.' Harry Leavis sat back in his chair and regarded Paul with serious concern. 'You said you were being pushed?'

'I've got Meedon and Trahearne of Serious Crimes on my back. I've a nasty feeling they may be trying to settle some old scores.'

'Those two bastards.' Leavis finished his brandy. 'You know, you're wasting your life on that wishy-washy non-aligned newspaper of yours. You should join the Party.'

Paul smiled. 'I prefer to keep to the middle of the road.'

'You'll get run over one of these days.'

'I'm pretty quick on my feet.'

'I hope so,' Leavis said. 'What's at the back of all this?'

Paul told him about the two suicides, his visit to Bloomsbury and his encounter with General Stapleton and Colonel Ferris. 'I want you to turn up anything you can on the sect, its contacts or affiliations with right-wing groups, particularly Excalibur – any detail, it doesn't matter how insignificant.'

'When do you need it?' Leavis asked.

'Could you get me something tonight?'

The man looked doubtful. 'I can try.'

'Good. I'll meet you back here about nine.'

'Not here.' Harry shook his head quickly. 'Never meet in the same place twice, you should know that.' He considered a moment. 'Battersea,' he said. 'The Marquis of Anglesey, little place at the bottom of Albert Bridge Road. Only don't turn up if you think you're being followed.'

'By Trahearne?'

'I wasn't thinking of Trahearne.' Leavis's small bright eyes fixed on Paul for a moment. 'You watch yourself now, laddie.'

He got up and left the table. He suffered from bunions and had slit his shoes to accommodate them. Walking on the outsides of his feet, his haversack over his shoulder, he went off across the bar with a quick hobbling gait.

Paul sat for a few minutes finishing his beer. Then he too left the pub.

He walked slowly through the blinding heat towards Notting Hill Underground. It was Wednesday, he recalled. On Friday he had his lunch date in the country with Diana Beresford. Near Newbury, a house called Woodlands, she had said. Suddenly he halted. For nearly a minute he stood staring in front of him. He was thinking of something Nicola had said to him at lunch last week. He moved on, heading briskly down the street now.

There were two telephone boxes near the Underground station. He went into the first one and found that the phone had been ripped from its panel. Entering the second, he searched for change. Someone had written 'Nigs Out. Pak Shit' on the wall above his head. He dialled his own number at the news room. 'Something about having failed and being "driven from green fields" ' Nicola had said, recalling her conversation with Rosamond in the station cafeteria. The bell rang for a long time at the other end. Finally Helen, his secretary, answered.

'Helen. This is Paul. Look, love, I want you to do something for me. I'm trying to to trace the whereabouts of a house in Berkshire, a large property that might have been bought about six months ago. It could be called Greenfields. Try the big London agents and any firm in Berkshire itself that might have handled the sale. It's very important – see what you can turn up.'

'Right away,' Helen said.

From Notting Hill Gate he took the Underground to Piccadilly. There was one visit he had to make on his way to Fleet Street. It was merely routine, like so much of the work he did on his stories; but he had long ago acquired the habit of thoroughness.

The Charity Commissioners occupied a suite of offices on the third floor of a building in the Haymarket. The clerk whom Paul interviewed was a rather superior young man wearing an elegantly cut gabardine suit and a garishly patterned kipper tie. He led his visitor to the central registry and showed him the file relating to the Regiment of God, Fifth Church of the Eternal Spirit, Coptic Street, Bloomsbury. Paul studied it carefully. The names of the officers of the sect, with the exception of General Anderton, meant nothing to him. There was no mention of any establishment in Berkshire, no address but the Bloomsbury one.

From the clerk he learned that charities were defined, according to a legal ruling of 1891, as being for the relief of poverty, the advancement of education and religion and other purposes beneficial to the community. In order to set up a charitable organisation the applicant had to produce a trust instrument stating who the parties were, the purpose of the organisation and how it was to be run. The principal advantages of charitable status were rate reliefs and exemption from taxes on voluntary donations.

Paul stood a moment frowning at the file. 'To what extent is the system open to abuses?' he asked. 'People saying they're going to do one thing and then carrying out some quite different activity?'

'There's no way of dunking a trust instrument like

litmus paper,' the young man replied loftily. 'But if the commissioners have any doubts, they can always insist on a solicitor's deed.' He took the file away from Paul, put it in the drawer and closed the cabinet firmly. 'I can assure you, they are in any case highly experienced at assessing the genuineness of applications.'

'I'm sure they are,' Paul said. 'Thank you for the information.'

David Plummer looked up suspiciously from a sheet of copy as Paul entered the news room and crossed to his desk.

Helen was waiting for him, a broad smile on her face. 'I found it for you,' she said. 'The house in Berkshire.'

'You're a wonder. Where is it?' He felt a sudden excitement.

'Five miles from Hungerford, outside a village called West Darton. The name *is* Greenfields. It's a big house standing in about forty acres of ground and was bought just over six months ago. The agents wouldn't tell me the name of the purchaser.'

'It doesn't matter.' Paul started away.

'Oh – there was a call for you just now . . .'

He stopped and looked round.

'A firm of solicitors. St Botolph's Yard, Bishopsgate. Ballard, Pilgrim & McNee. Mr Ballard wanted to see you. He said it was very urgent. Would this afternoon or tomorrow morning do?'

'What do they want?'

'He wouldn't say.'

Paul stood thinking a moment. He had never heard of Ballard, Pilgrim or McNee. 'Tell them I'll go along in the morning about ten,' he said.

Heading for the door, he passed Plummer who was coming towards him extracting a biscuit from a packet in his hand. 'You're in a great hurry,' the News Editor said.

'There's a mad dog got loose in Berkshire,' Paul

told him.

As he went on out of the room, he was gratified to hear Plummer choking on his biscuit.

Greenfields turned out to be a large redbrick mansion standing at the head of a gravel driveway about a mile from the village of West Darton. Paul had stopped to make a few inquiries around the village but had learned little. The house was locally believed to be a business training college run by an American corporation the name of which nobody seemed to know. None of the students or teachers had ever been seen in the village and none of the tradespeople, not even the newsagent, did business with the house.

Heading up the driveway, he was impressed by the quietness of the place. There wasn't a soul to be seen in the grounds, no sign of movement anywhere, the windows of the mansion staring blankly at him in the sunlight. Stopping the car at the foot of the entrance steps, he got out and looked around him. A flock of rooks circled the tops of some oak trees near the border of the property; a magpie rose from the lawn in front of him and went flapping away into the distance. Not a sound broke the hot, hazy silence of the afternoon. Climbing the steps to the black-painted front door, he rang the bell.

For several minutes nothing happened. The magpie came back, landed briefly on the driveway and took off again.

At last he heard a faint sound of footsteps and the door opened. Facing him was a young man wearing a navy-blue blazer, a white shirt and tie and dark grey-flannel trousers. His hair was cut very short, his manner cautious and alert. 'Good afternoon, sir,' he said. 'What can I do for you?'

'My name's Paul Marriott. I'm a journalist. This is the training college of the Regiment of God?'

The young man simply looked at him, neither confirming nor denying the fact. 'What is the nature of your business, sir?' he asked in the same coldly formal voice.

'I want to talk to someone about Rosamond Clay and Jack Tendler.'

The other's face remained perfectly blank. If he were acting, Paul thought, then it was an exceedingly good performance.

At that moment there were more footsteps and another youth appeared. He was dressed in the same way; except that on the breast pocket of his blazer there was embroidered the mailed-fist emblem of the Regiment of God, probably indicating that he was of higher status than the other youth. Paul recognized him at once. It was the young man who had delivered the sermon at the St Catherine's Hall prayer meeting.

'Good afternoon, sir,' the youngster said, his sharp lean face icy and unsmiling. 'Can I be of any help? My name is Walter.'

'Walter?'

'We don't use family names here, sir.' The boy looked briefly at his companion. 'This is Robert.'

'I was just telling Robert,' Paul said, 'I'm interested in two former members of your sect – Rosamond Clay and Jack Tendler.'

Walter shook his head. He had a maddeningly supercilious air about him, a look of frigid contempt in his flat, marksman's eyes. 'The names would mean nothing to me, sir. You see, the forenames we use are given to us when we join the Church. We know our sisters and brothers by no other names.'

'Is that so? The sister and brother I'm speaking of committed suicide a while ago. I feel sure the news must have reached you.'

There was a momentary silence. Walter threw a quick look at Robert, who turned and went away across the hall. Facing Paul again, the young preacher said, 'I'm afraid I know nothing about the matter. But if you'd care to step

124

into the office for a minute . . .'

'Thank you.' Paul passed through the doorway and Walter led him across a large, bare, white-painted hall. There was a huge portrait of General Anderton on one wall, flanked by two banners. The first banner bore the legend: 'Stretch out your sickle and reap, for the harvest-time has come and the crop is overripe'; the second said: 'This is the hour of victory for our God, the hour of his sovereignty and power'.

The office was similarly austere: a green metal desk, metal filing cabinets and wooden chairs; another portrait of the general, this time surmounted by an American flag and a Union Jack. Paul wasn't asked to sit down.

'I must explain that interviews are never given to journalists without prior appointment,' Walter informed him, 'and then only at the Coptic Street office.'

'You seem to keep this place a pretty closely guarded secret,' Paul observed.

'No, sir, we do not. On the other hand we don't advertise its existence.' He looked insolently at Paul for a moment. 'We don't want the rabble coming to our door.' Turning, he walked to a cupboard in the corner. 'If you want an interview, you can fill in an application form and take it to our Bloomsbury office. I should point out though that all copy written by journalists must be submitted to the Church's Press Officer before publication.' He took a form from the cupboard, came back and handed it to Paul.

Paul glanced at the document; it was a two-page, printed questionnaire. 'Looks more like a visa application for the People's Republic of China,' he said.

Walter wasn't amused. 'You can file the application or not, as you choose, sir.'

Just then a door opened across the hall and a man appeared wearing a dark blue track suit and plimsolls. He came towards the office at a brisk, measured pace as if he were marching across a parade ground. Entering the room, he nodded to Walter, who departed and closed the door behind him.

The newcomer was around forty years of age with sparse reddish hair, his almost perfectly round face pale and slightly freckled. His mouth was small, his lips very red, the lower one stuck out in an aggressive and belligerent fashion. He stood against the door for a moment, perfectly still and very erect, staring fixedly at Paul through a pair of bright blue, rather protruding eyes.

'My name is Bernard Larke,' he said in a firm, quiet voice. 'I'm in charge here.' Crossing the room, he went behind the desk. 'Walter will have told you about our rules covering interviews to the press.'

'Yes. I can see you don't encourage visitors,' Paul said. 'But I got your address from Rosamond Clay.'

The piece of bluff produced no visible reaction from the man in the track suit. The slightly bulging blue eyes remained distant and hostile. 'We're not permitted to discuss the affairs of members of the Church, past or present,' he said. 'It's another of our rules.'

'I quite understand,' Paul said. 'I imagine your course here must be pretty demanding. You have to expect some failures.'

'Many are called but few are chosen,' Bernard Larke replied unctuously.

'How many? What's your drop-out rate?'

'There again, it's a subject I can't discuss, sir.'

'I thought there must have been more than two since you opened this place six months ago. I was wondering what happened to the others?'

There was a little silence. Larke continued to stand motionless behind the desk. 'What others?' he asked in a soft and faintly menacing tone. 'We're doing God's work here. We're his servants, the chosen instruments of his grand design. The way of the Lord is steep and narrow, and stony is the path. If some fall by the wayside, it's only to be expected.'

126

'It was a long fall though, wasn't it, for Rosamond Clay?' Paul walked to one of the windows and stood a moment looking down the driveway. 'What do you do with your backsliders? Put them through some kind of psychological wringer?' He turned round. 'The Music Room. Isn't that what you call it?'

Larke's expression didn't change. Only his lower lip protruded just a shade more and a suspicion of colour showed on his pale cheeks. Then all at once he seemed to relax a little. Leaving the desk, he started to walk about the room. He became suddenly almost effusive. Evidently Paul had succeeded in shaking him. 'We've no secrets here – nothing to hide, I assure you,' he siad. 'It's all laid down in the general's books and in our various pamphlets and publications. Anyone can study them who's interested. Only we believe our seminars are best conducted in the privacy of this house, out of the way of the mob.' He gave a grimace of a smile, his frog-like eyes as cruelly cold as ever. 'The little grey souls, the mongrel populace,' he added disdainfully. ' "For wheresoever the rabble drink, all wells are poisoned." '

'May I ask what these seminars consist of?' Paul inquired.

Larke went on pacing the room. 'Reorientation, purification, dedication,' he said in a flat, impersonal tone. 'As set out in the general's manual. The youngsters learn to serve. To give and not to grab. To cease to be blowflies, parasites and ambitious scramblers. We produce cadres of young people, trained in all manner of skills, ready to assist the authorities in time of need. Devotedly, efficiently and in the name of the Lord.'

'In time of need,' Paul said. 'What need?'

'In the event of civil strife, sir. Or any national emergency.'

'Involving the mongrel populace?'

Larke only smiled, a single gold tooth glinting in his upper jaw.

'And where do you recruit these youngsters?' Paul asked.

'From the highways and byways, like the Master himself.'

'Only rather more discreetly.'

' "The spirit grows best in solitude. You raise young eagles in harsh and lonely places. The flames moke and turn foul when the rabble approach the fire." ' He turned, a disturbingly intent look on his face. ' "Are poisoned wells needed, and stinking fires, and maggots in the bread of life?" '

'The general's words?' Paul asked.

'Neetchee,' Larke said.

For a moment Paul was puzzled. Nietzsche? Friedrich Neitzsche? The nineteenth-century German philosopher who had preached the cult of the Superman; the ideal of a master race dwelling like eagles above morality and the principles of good and evil. A thinker considered by many to have been the grandfather of Naziism. 'Friedrich Neitzsche?' he said. 'I thought he was an atheist.'

Larke shook his head. 'You should read the general's writings. He makes everything clear. There's a lot about Neetchee—how he was a voice crying in the wilderness, making straight the way of the Lord. It's all in there. It's all laid down.'

He turned and started back towards the desk. In the ensuing silence they both heard a sound coming from somewhere behind the house. The measured tread of marching feet. Larke paused and crossed to a window that looked out on the rear of the property. Paul followed him.

A short distance away was a broad expanse of lawn on which stood a flag-pole hung with the Union Jack. Approaching along a gravel path in three perfectly straight ranks were about fifty young people. Most of them were boys, some dozen girls in blue blazers and grey skirts bringing up the rear. At a command from the leader of the column, the contingent executed a precise right

128

wheel and came marching across the grass. Here they halted, arrayed like soldiers before the flag-pole. The young men, Paul noticed, were carrying pick handles at their sides.

For a few seconds Larke stood, hands behind his back, staring through the window. Looking beyond the lawn towards the middle distance, Paul glimpsed what appeared to be a raised cat-walk running among some trees, a rope hanging from a branch at the end. Evidently part of an assault course, he decided. Over to his right, again partly hidden by the trees, was a brick wall some twenty feet high by thirty feet long; standing isolated at the head of a clearing, it appeared to serve no useful purpose. Unless, he thought suddenly, it were the butt of a rifle range.

'My young Ironsides,' Larke said with a note of pride in his voice. Then he moved to the door and held it open for Paul. 'The daily inspection, sir.'

'Very impressive,' Paul said as he joined him in the doorway. 'What are the pick handles for?'

'Mainly drill purposes, sir. The young men also receive some training in riot control.'

As they crossed the hall Paul observed another banner hanging above the front door. 'This is our height and our home. Too high and too steep dwell we here for the unclean and their thirsts.'

Larke opened the door. 'Good-bye, Mr Marriott,' he said. 'May God go with you.'

'Amen,' Paul replied.

As he descended the steps he was surprised to see a highly polished and very military-looking Land-Rover parked behind his car. One of Larke's young Ironsides was at the wheel. Seated beside him, erect and very much on duty, was Walter.

Climbing into his Triumph, Paul drove off. After a moment the Land-Rover followed.

It remained twenty-five yards beh'nd him all the way

along the road through West Darton and on to Newbury. Only when he entered the town did he lose his escort, the Land-Rover slowing and turning into a side-road.

Altogether it had been a bizarre and somewhat theatrical encounter, he reflected. What he couldn't quite decide was whether Bernard Larke had been giving a performance or whether he was indeed more than a little mad.

Just after nine o'clock that night he stopped his car outside the Marquis of Anglesey at the bottom of Albert Bridge Road. Mindful of Leavis's warning, he sat for a minute or two looking in the driving mirror. No other car pulled up behind him; no figure could be seen lurking in the shadows along the pavement. It seemed unlikely that he had been followed. Getting out of the car, he went into the pub.

Harry was sitting at a corner table in the nearly deserted bar. Beside him was a man in a grey suit who must have weighed every bit of twenty stone. He was in his middle years, dark-skinned, with a big beak of a nose and heavily lidded eyes.

'This is Gabriel,' Harry said as Paul came over. 'Mr Marriott.'

The man called Gabriel nodded, this many chins creasing over his collar, his look guarded and appraising. Harry's glass was empty as usual. The stranger had an untouched half-pint of bitter in front of him. 'I'll get some drinks,' Paul said. Picking up Harry's glass, he went to the bar.

He didn't like the look of Gabriel. Arab, or more probably Levantine, he was certainly no street corner communist stooge. The man had a certain air of authority about him, something subtly impressive, cold and even dangerous. What function he might perform in the complex, subterranean world of international terrorism would have been anybody's guess. Paul had an ugly, instinctive feeling that he was getting himself into deep water. Picking up the drinks, he went back and sat down.

'I told Gabriel about your interest in the Excalibur Society,' Harry said. 'I think perhaps he can give you a few pointers.'

The fat man stirred in his chair, looked distastefully at his half-pint and pushed the glass away from him. 'I'll be happy to tell you anything I can,' he said in a low, quiet voice. 'Though unfortunately I know nothing about the religious sect Mr Leavis mentioned.' He sat a moment, twisting a huge gold ring on his right forefinger. He seemed to be in no hurry. Paul waited. 'The Excalibur Society itself requires little explanation. Far more interesting is their fellow organization, the Confederation for International Studies. Mr Leavis tells me you already know a little about them, how they have links with British intelligence and some very highly placed people in the Foreign Office, not to mention the CIA. The Confederation is in fact an intelligence service within an intelligence service. Though its function is supposed to be purely academic, it works closely and sometimes actively with SI5 and SI6.' Gabriel sat frowning to himself for a moment. 'A think-tank – and a very deep one – it commands the services of some of the most able brains in the country, soldiers, scientists, even a former deputy director of SIS: a new breed of dedicated military thinkers, you understand, far removed from the much-caricatured upper-class fool of an officer of old. More, you might say, in the spirit of James Bond than Colonel Blimp. Men who are busily concentrating their minds on such fundamental and far-reaching questions as the relationship between the civil and the military power in an era of ever more violent political and racial conflict. The architects, we would say, of a new fascism.'

Having delivered his lecture, Gabriel paused. Paul noticed that Harry's glass was already empty, but he didn't feel inclined to get up and refill it. Up to now it seemed that Gabriel had only been trying to impress him.

He was deeply curious to know what the real point of the meeting might be.

'As I told you, I know nothing about the Regiment of God,' Gabriel continued. 'Though men like General Stapleton and Colonel Ferris would in all likelihood approve of General Anderton's programme and be inclined to give him support.' He turned to Paul. 'You were looking for some link, am I right, between Anderton's church and the Excalibur Society?'

'There has to be one,' Paul said.

Gabriel nodded. 'I was particularly interested in what Mr Leavis told me about the psychological condition of this young girl,' he said slowly. 'Rosamond – what was it?'

'Clay.'

The big man sat for a few seconds meditatively twisting the ring on his finger. 'Might I ask you to tell me again, in your own words, exactly how she appeared to be?'

His puzzlemen growing, Paul proceeded to describe Rosamond's condition in as much detail as he could.

'And you formed no theory yourself as to what might have happened to her?' Gabriel asked when he had finished.

'None. I talked to a doctor about it. He could suggest no explanation.'

'Now . . . I'm sorry to impose on you to this extent, Mr Marriott. But could I ask you to repeat everything you know about the Regiment of God? I gather from Mr Leavis that your paper has quite a bit of background on them.'

Paul thought quickly. He would tell Gabriel only what he had already told Harry. He would say nothing about his visit to Greenfields. Far from receiving any information from the man across the table, he had clearly been brought here only to answer questions. The discovery disturbed him. He felt more than ever that there was a need for caution. He described his encounter with Skeggs at the Coptic Street office and how he had gone to the prayer meeting; also his conversation with the reporter Barry Hellman in the news room the previous week. Finishing his story, he paused. Then on a sudden impulse he added, 'We think there might be somebody involved called Bernard Larke. I don't know if the name means anything to you?'

Gabriel had been staring down at the table. He raised his head now and looked at Harry. Then he turned slowly to Paul. 'Bernard Larke?' he repeated. 'What makes you believe he's connected with the Regiment of God?'

Paul shrugged. 'The name came up when I was talking to Hellman. I only wondered if you'd ever heard of him.'

'Oh yes, I've heard of him all right,' Gabriel said. He was looking closely at Paul. 'You didn't meet him, then?'

'He wasn't at Coptic Street. But Barry did a lot of ferreting around, talked to a great many people. I think he heard the name mentioned at one of the sect meetings.'

Gabriel's heavy-lidded eyes were searching Paul's face, as a man might look for a dropped pin on a carpet. 'You didn't tell me Mr Hellman had attended any meetings.'

'He went to one or two. Is it important?'

Gabriel turned his head away, sat back in his chair and gave a little sigh. 'I'm sorry. You must think I'm being very ungracious. You've been most helpful and I shouldn't be cross-examining you.' He paused, pondering a moment. 'Perhaps I can do you a favour in return. The information you've given me suggests one or two lines of inquiry that I can pursue during the next twenty-four hours. After I've talked to a few people, I might be able to supply you with some of the background you need.' He smiled. 'I'd like to assist you if I can. I don't disapprove of your newspaper. It's bourgeois, but it does display a certain social objectivity. May I suggest we meet again tomorrow? Not in a public place. A flat in Bayswater, if that would be convenient to you. Chepstow House, Craven Square. Number Five on the second floor. Say, about this time?'

133

'I'll be there,' Paul said.

'Good. And thank you for being so patient.'

Paul looked briefly at Harry and caught a faintly alarmed expression in his eyes.

He got up. 'I'll see you tomorrow, then,' he said to Gabriel. Nodding to the two men, he left the pub.

He hadn't eaten since breakfast. After returning from Greenfields he had spent three hours working on Merlin's accursed rabies story. The piece wasn't coming out very well, but no matter; Plummer didn't want it until late on Friday.

Going to the kitchen, he took some ham from the fridge to make himself a sandwich. As he went to collect the bread from the larder, he put his head into the scullery. The night breeze was blowing warm through the open window above the mews. Fred had not returned.

He had just finished making the sandwich when the telephone rang.

Carrying the plate to his study, he picked up the receiver.

'Paul – this is Harry.' Leavis's high-pitched voice sounded strained.

'Yes, Harry?'

'For God's sake, lad – you're not keeping that appointment tomorrow night?'

'I know. It stinks, doesn't it? But I may have to take a chance.'

'Don't be a damned fool. You're in enough trouble as it is.' The old man sounded a little breathless in his agitation. 'You want to finish up being measured for a coffin?'

'One thing at a time,' Paul said. 'First – what's all this about Bernard Larke?'

'I'll tell you about Bernard Larke,' Leavis replied. 'He was a sergeant-major in the Special Air Service. He was discharged a year ago, officially on medical grounds – in fact because he was considered to be emotionally unstable.'

There was a brief pause while Leavis caught his breath. 'By all accounts, he's more than half-way round the bend. He caused grave embarrassment to the authorities during his last tour of duty in Northern Ireland, principally because of his over-enthusiasm in the treatment and interrogation of prisoners. Need I say more?'

'I get the picture,' Paul said.

'There are plenty of boyos in London at this moment who'd give anything in the world to get their hands on Bernie Larke. You've put the cat among the pigeons, lad. You told Gabriel you didn't know where Larke was. He doesn't believe you. Nor will anybody else. And that's only half your troubles.'

'Tell me the other half,' Paul said.

Nothing but Harry's wheezing breath came over the line for a moment. 'Rosamond Clay,' he said finally, 'and what was done to her.'

'She was driven mad.'

'There's a bloody sight more to it than that.' Harry's voice sounded shrill. 'Get any deeper into this business and your life won't be worth a damn. I can't help you any more, you understand? Take my advice, go pack a bag and disappear for a while. Take a month's holiday, lose yourself. . . .'

'A story's a story, Harry . . .'

'There's no story. Not a word your paper could ever print. Think about what I've said, boy, or you'll be sorry.'

The line went dead. Replacing the receiver, Paul sat down at his desk and pushed the plate away from him. He had suddenly lost his appetite. Frowning to himself, he tried to recall what he knew about the Special Air Service. A wartime commando unit trained to operate far behind the enemy lines, it had been disbanded in 1945 and then reformed as part of the regular army around 1950. Significantly, the SAS had received very little press coverage until a group of them had been sent to Northern

Ireland a year ago. Trained as they were to operate as much like secret agents as soldiers, they had always occupied a somewhat nebulous position in the sphere of military activities. He had little doubt that departments like SI5 and SI6 made frequent use of SAS personnel in their undercover work. Clearly, a warrant officer like Larke would know a great deal about such things. He would also be an expert on interrogation methods as practised by our own side and by the enemy.

He sighed and sat back in his chair. Harry Leavis was probably right. He should drop the story like the hot potato, or the unexploded bomb, that it was. Then he thought of Rosamond Clay lying dead under his window; of the frightened faces of her parents; the anguish and bewilderment in the eyes of Jack Tendler's father; the young men lined up before the flag-pole at Greenfields with pick handles at their sides. . . .

To reach the offices of Ballard, Pilgrim & McNee, you had to ascend in a creaking cage lift to the top floor of an ancient building overlooking St Botolph's Yard at the eastern end of Bishopsgate.

The contraption shuddered to a halt and Paul stepped gratefully into the solicitors' outer office. He had expected something Dickensian; instead he found himself in the reception area of what could have been a fashionable advertising agency: the walls hung with maize-coloured fabric and decorated with three very presentable abstract paintings; the carpet a dark brown; the woodwork of polished pine.

A pretty girl greeted him with a smile and led him straight to Mr Ballard's office.

The office was also modern: the same wall coverings, another large abstract painting, Scandinavian-style furniture and two off-white leather armchairs for clients. A broad window filling most of the end wall and providing a magnificent view of St Paul's had the effect of making the room look like an expensive film set.

Mr Ballard, a frail and distinguished-looking man of about sixty, came forward to shake hands. 'Mr Marriott, good morning,' he said. 'How good of you to come along. May I introduce Mr Milner?'

Mr Milner was standing by one of the armchairs. A little younger than Ballard, he was short and belligerent-looking, with a bulldog face and curly fair hair. He greeted Paul with a curt nod and a swiftly appraising look.

The three of them sat down, Ballard behind the desk.

'I'll come straight to the point,' Mr Milner said to Paul. 'You published a small item in your newspaper last week concerning the deaths of two young people who had been members of a certain religious sect. Unfortunately the item was only brought to my notice yesterday. When I read it, I promptly called Mr Ballard. We both decided that you could very probably be of help to us.'

Ballard folded his hands on the desk and leaned forward. 'Mr Milner and I are joint executors of the Antonia Unwin Trust,' he said, speaking slowly and softly. 'Antonia Unwin, a niece of Mr Milner's, inherited a large sum of money from her father about a year ago. Quite recently, somewhat to our dismay, she joined the Regiment of God.' The man sat back, a slim, dark figure against the City skyline. 'Now, to our more profound dismay, she has decided to donate her fortune to this – ah – religious body. In principle, the trust is binding for her lifetime. Legally, however, there is very little we could do to prevent her breaking it when she attains the age of twenty-five.' The solicitor leaned forward again, looking earnestly at Paul. 'As executors, we're empowered to exercise our discretion in the matter only if it can be proved that the sect is engaged in criminal, subversive or illegal activities. Do I make myself clear?'

'Perfectly clear,' Paul said.

'Mr Marriott,' Milner turned to Paul. 'You may name any fee you like. Any sum at all. In return, would you be prepared to give your time exclusively to the investigation of this religious sect on our behalf? I should add that we wouldn't need your services for long. There is, unfortunately, very little time.'

'I'm already working on the story pretty well exclusively for my newspaper,' Paul said. 'Though understandably they're a little chary of the subject. As you probably know, there are some very influential people concerned, at least indirectly, with the Regiment of God.'

'Yes, we do know that,' Milner said.

'Excalibur?' Paul asked. 'General Stapleton?'

Ballard nodded to him across the desk. The general's son, Claude Stapleton, is Antonia Unwin's banker. It was he who introduced her to the sect.'

There was a brief silence. Paul sat thinking. 'There's no question of my accepting a fee from you,' he said. 'If I turn up any incriminating evidenceand—I haven't done so yet—you'd be perfectly welcome to it.' He looked round at Milner. 'When does your niece become twenty-five?'

Milner looked over at the window. 'We have until midnight tomorrow,' he said quietly.

'May I ask how much money is involved?' Paul inquired.

Milner was still gazing steadily at the window. 'Five million pounds,' he replied.

Faintly, Paul heard the lift go rumbling down the well across the building. Several things had immediately become clear to him. Not least the anxiety of General Stapleton and Colonel Ferris to keep him from prying into the affairs of the Regiment of God – even to the extent of planting false evidence with the police, and possibly using their influence at the Yard, to suggest that he had murdered Rosamond Clay. The lift came to a stop. Five million pounds. The thought of such a vast, untaxable fortune in the hands of a near-mad man like Bernard Larke was sobering indeed.

'One suggestion,' Milner was saying. 'We've been

employing the services of a private detective for some weeks now, a man called Arthur Frewin. It might be useful if you were to meet him.'

'A good idea,' Paul said. 'I'd be glad to.'

'This morning?'

'I don't see why not.'

Ballard picked up a telephone and asked to be put through to Mr Frewin. He talked briefly to the man, then got up and came round the desk. 'He'll see you in half an hour,' he said to Paul, giving him the address.

Paul walked with Ballard and Milner to the door. 'You may find Mr Frewin a little unconventional,' Milner said. 'But I've been assured he's one of the best men in his field.'

Paul nodded. He felt sure that Mr Milner would employ no one but the best.

Arthur Frewin was a rotund and genial little man with sparkling blue eyes and sandy hair. He ran his business from a small ground-floor flat in Cromwell Road. A back room with French windows opening on to a walled patio served as his office. There appeared to be no dividing line between his professional and his domestic activities; the two were carried on simultaneously and in an atmosphere of disorder and confusion which must have bewildered his clients but which seemed to trouble Frewin not at all.

His two children, a girl and a boy of seven and eight, were playing noisily in a paddle pool outside the French windows while his wife, a large and placid woman in a bathing costume, shelled peas in a deck chair near by. The room itself was so cluttered that there was scarcely space to move or sit down: newspapers, files, books, boxes filled with correspondence, dusty magazines and children's toys covered nearly every available surface. Removing a plastic dinosaur and volume twelve of the *Encyclopaedia Britannica* from a corner of the sofa, Paul found himself a seat. While the children shrieked outside and jet-liners thundered over the rooftops at the rate of about one a

minute, he gave Frewin a detailed account of his investi-
gations, finishing with Harry Leavis's telephone call the
previous evening.

Frewin listened carefully, picking his way about the
debris-strewn floor and nodding his head from time
to time.

When Paul had finished, he stood frowning a moment,
swaying back and forth on his feet. 'The suicides. Don't
know what to make of it. Brainwashing. A drug? Yes, very
probably a drug.' He had a quick, laconic way of speaking, like a man dictating telegrams. 'Larke did some
courses at Porton Down, chemical warfare place.
Know that?'

'No, I didn't,' Paul said.

'Dossier on him.' Frewin crossed the room and pulled
a sheet of paper from the bulging drawer of a filing
cabinet. 'Difficult job. Ministry of Defence as tight as
clams. His last posting was an interrogation centre in
Armagh. That's where he got into trouble. There . . .'

Paul took the sheet of paper. Frewin had done a remark-
ably thorough job on the errant sergeant-major. As he had
suspected, Larke was widely experienced in every aspect
of security and counter-insurgency work. He had specia-
lised as an interrogator and had been twice to
Porton Down.

'Went to Greenfields myself,' Frewin was saying.
'Couldn't get in. Quite impossible. Interesting what you
say about it.' He continued to walk round the room,
meditatively pushing a toy fire engine with the toe of his
shoe. 'I kept an eye on Coptic Street for some time. Agree
it's largely a front. Also I think Skeggs is in charge of
recruiting. Runs a group of agents, some American,
mostly British. They work the pubs and discos around
west London, looking for likely kids – drop-outs, drifters.
The novices do a short training at Coptic Street. Only the
more suitable ones find their way to Greenfields. Little or
no contact with the outside world after that. As in the

general's American churches, the kids are no doubt obliged to renounce all loyalties to home, family and friends.'

'Daddy! Daddy! Nigel's throwing stones in the pool!' The little girl was jumping up and down in the garden doorway.

'Come here, Alice,' her mother called. 'Daddy's with a client.'

'Daddy's with a client! Daddy's with a client!' The girl turned and ran off across the patio.

Frewin brought the fire engine to a stop in front of an empty cat basket on the floor. Looking through the window, it seemed to Paul that Nigel was making a determined attempt to drown his little sister. Mrs Frewin, paying not the slightest attention, went on shelling the peas.

'I agree Larke must be putting pressure on the parents of the two dead youngsters,' Frewin said. 'Probably threatening the safety of Nicola Clay and the two other Tendler children. One thing to suggest that, another thing to prove it.' He picked up the fire engine, examined it briefly and put it back on the floor. 'There you are. Have to admit I've come to a dead end.'

'I'm going to take a chance and keep that appointment with Gabriel tonight,' Paul said. 'Meanwhile there's another line you could follow. John Aubrey, Rosamond Clay's boy friend. I got the impression that day he knew more than he pretended. He's a junkie, he might even be a registered addict, so it shouldn't be too difficult to find him.'

'Piccadilly, the all-night chemist, subway four, the "meat rack".' Frewin was referring to that section of the Piccadilly subway frequented by addicts; the 'meat rack' were the arches on the north side of the Circus where youngsters went to beg and prostitute themselves for the price of a fix. Evidently the man knew his way around. 'No problem,' he said. 'Leave it to me. Description?'

Paul gave him as accurate a description as he could of John Aubrey.

'I'll be on to it right away,' Frewin said. A bright yellow rubber duck came sailing through the window; he caught it deftly and tossed it back into the pool. 'I'll find him, don't worry.'

Paul got to his feet. Nigel was holding his sister's head underwater again. He exchanged telephone numbers with Frewin, called good-bye to the woman in the deck chair and left.

The stairwell of the Mansion block seemed even hotter than usual as he made his way up to the fourth floor. There was a new piece of graffiti on the third landing. Someone had simply written 'HELP' in large letters across the wall. To Paul, it seemed a fairly appropriate motto for the week. Sweating, he climbed on.

The three men on the next floor must have heard him coming. They had turned and were waiting with their backs to the door of the flat as he approached. Chief Inspector Trahearne, looking more than ever as if he were on loan from the KGB, stood between the young cat-faced detective and another man whom Paul hadn't seen before.

'Good morning, Mr Marriott,' Trahearne said woodenly as Paul reached the landing. 'May we have another word with you?'

Paul produced his keys and let them into the flat.

'I'd like to look at your study again, if I may, sir,' Trahearne said as Paul closed the front door.

'By all means. Come along.' Paul led the way down the passage. Trahearne and the young detective followed, the other man remaining behind.

The study window was still open. Trahearne crossed the room, his companion again standing like a sentry at the door. The Chief Inspector looked down out of the window and up at the parapet as he had done before.

Then he turned to face Paul. 'I've been studying the forensic report on Miss Clay,' he said. 'Apparently she could have fallen from any height between fifty and sixty feet.

Paul merely waited. In the area he could hear Mr Kolokowski emptying his rubbish bin. The distance between the window ledge and the parapet would be just about ten feet, he reckoned.

'The report also indicated that she'd been in the habit of using drugs,' Trahearne went on.

'Yes. John Aubrey told me she'd been taken amphetamines – purple hearts,' Paul said. 'By the way, have you made any effort to find him?'

The only reply he got was a coldly hostile look from Trahearne. There was a silence as the detective came a little way across the room. 'It would be true to say, wouldn't it, sir, that you were pretty familiar with the world of drug addicts?'

'I've written some newspaper stories on the suject, yes.'

'You'd know the places frequented by these people. Possibly you've kept up some association with them since you wrote your articles. What I'm suggesting is that you could quite easily have picked up a young woman like Miss Clay in Piccadilly or Romilly Street.'

'I could have picked her up on Hampstead Heath,' Paul said.

Trahearne walked to the desk. He stood a moment, looking down into a bowl of paper-clips as if he were counting them. 'It's true though, isn't it, that you have quite a success with the young ladies?'

'I'm the busiest ram in Fleet Street. Ask anyone.'

The Chief Inspector looked up, his face as hard as stone. 'One might go so far as to say that there'd been a steady succession of young women coming in and out of this flat over the years.'

'It would be no exaggeration,' Paul said. Probably Trahearne had been talking to the Kolokowskis. Also, he thought, the police would have had no difficulty in tracing the sacked porter.

'Furthermore you're a man not unaccustomed to using violence.' Trahearne had turned and was looking towards the window again.

'You mean, the Chinese gangster I'm supposed to have bashed in Soho – when I got warned off the manor?'

'There have been other occasions, sir. An affray in Southall. . . .' Trahearne was still standing with his back to the desk. He took a few paces forward, seeming to measure the floorspace between the desk and the window. 'You're a judo expert, is that right, Mr Marriott?'

'Karate.'

The Chief Inspector turned. 'A girl like Miss Clay now . . . A girl off the streets, as it were. Needing a supply of drugs, needing money, needing shelter. . . . If you'd taken her in, she might have thought she was on to a good thing. She'd be difficult to get rid off. She might become troublesome. You see what I mean, sir?'

Paul was suddenly tired of Trahearne. He felt his temper beginning to snap. 'For the love of Christ! If I was going to murder Rosamond Clay, you really think I would have thrown her out of that window in broad daylight?' Going to his chair, he sat down, put his elbows on the desk and looked hard at the detective. 'It's a load of balls and you know it.'

'We've received certain information and we're obliged to act on it, sir,' Trahearne said formally.

'You've received information! Come off it, Trahearne!' Paul raised his voice suddenly. 'You're out for my guts – you're trying to work a fit-up on me. You, Commander Meedon and a bunch of highly placed crypto-fascist shit-heads who want to shut my mouth at any price. Don't tell me Meedon hasn't been put up to this, because I know bloody well he has. And if you like I'll tell you who the shit-heads are protecting. His name is Bernard Larke and at this moment he's training a private army in a house

144

called Greenfields near the village of West Darton outside Newbury. It was Larke who got at Rosamond Clay and drove her to suicide. And I'll tell you another thing. Maniacs like Larke could be running this country one of these days if people like you and Meedon don't stop frigging around and go back to doing your jobs – enforcing the law instead of pursuing idiotic vendettas and licking the arses of fascist piss-willies like General Stapleton and Colonel Ferris.'

Trahearne stood motionless for a long moment. His face had reddened; his black, slitted eyes had almost disappeared behind the folds of his fleshy cheeks; there were little white flecks at the corners of his mouth. 'These are pretty wild charges, sir,' he said in a dead, quiet voice.

'I mean to substantiate them.' Paul sat back, making an effort to calm himself. 'I've someone out now looking for John Aubrey. When he's found he'll be able to testify that Rosamond Clay was living in the attic here for a whole week up to the day she died.'

'A heroin addict?' Trahearne looked at him contemptuously. 'A boy who'd say anything for a few quid?' He walked away a few paces and stood frowning at the *Guernica* reproduction on the wall. 'It puzzles me that you should lay so much stress on the Aubrey kid. Surely there must be other people, friends of yours, who visited you that week and would be able to provide testimony.'

Paul said nothing for a moment. The Chief Inspector had turned and was watching him. 'There's nobody,' Paul said finally. 'I took the week off from my paper. I was writing a piece for an American magazine. I shut myself away. I didn't see anyone.'

Trahearne fastened the middle button of his jacket. He seemed to relax all at once. 'Well now, that's a little unfortunate, isn't it, sir?' he said softly.

Without looking at Paul again, he went out of the room with the young detective. Paul got up and followed.

As he went along the passage he saw the other man, the

man who had come with Trahearne, standing in the living room. Moving on to the hall, he opened the front door and watched the two detectives go down the stairs. Then he made his way to the front room.

Had he encountered the stranger under any other circumstances, he might have supposed that he was some kind of intellectual; a schoolmaster perhaps. The man wasn't particularly well-dressed, his brown light-weight suit baggy and a little crumpled, his tie carelessly knotted; his hair was untidy, the overlong sideburns in need of a trim. His rather narrow face, grey and somehow tired-looking, did not seem unfriendly.

'I must apologise for walking into your home without introducing myself,' the man said quietly. 'But I thought it better to let Trahearne finish his business with you first. My name is Conran, Victor Conran. I wanted to talk to you about Rosamond Clay.'

'Won't you sit down?'

Comran moved to an armchair by the hearth.

Paul sat down opposite him. 'I take it you're not a policeman,' he said.

'No.' The man crossed his legs, revealing a pair of fallen grey socks. 'There's a certain aspect of this matter which might be of interest to Her Majesty's Government.'

'What aspect?'

'The notebooks. Rosamond Clay's notebooks.'

'I've already been over that with Trahearne.'

'Yes, I know.' Conran's tired, almost colourless eyes searched Paul's face. 'But somewhere there are at least two notebooks belonging to this girl. For reasons I can't discuss we're very anxious to get a sight of them.'

Paul said nothing for a moment. It had suddenly occurred to him to tell Conran about his meeting with Nicola Clay. He hesitated, however. Arthur Frewin had suggested that both Nicola and the Tendler children might be under some threat from the Regiment of God. The last thing he wanted was to put Nicola in danger. It was far from certain, in any case, that she could have told Conran anything useful. 'What makes you so sure these books exist?' he asked.

It was Conran's turn to consider. After a moment he said, 'There's no reason why I shouldn't tell you. It was mere chance. The police were at Mr and Mrs Clay's house last week, breaking the news about the girl's death. During the conversation the telephone rang. Mr Clay answered it. He listened for a minute or two then seemed to become rather agitated. He told the caller he knew nothing about his daughter's affairs, that he wasn't going to be threatened or pestered, and put down the phone. You must remember the police were dealing with the unexplained suicide of a young person, or conceivably with a murder. They questioned Mr Clay about the call. With some reluctance he told them it was from an anonymous man offering to sell him some notebooks belonging to his daughter. Next thing, you appear on the scene, return one notebook and question the Clays about the possible existence of others.'

'I was interested in the idea of getting her verses published,' Paul said.

Conran simply looked at him with frank disbelief.

'You think these books might contain an account of her experiences at Greenfields?' Paul asked finally.

'I'm afraid I can't go into that.'

'But you know what happened to her?'

Again the man didn't answer. Rising from his chair, he started across the room.

'You know bloody well I didn't kill her.' Paul was on his feet.

Conran stopped near the door and turned round. 'We want those notebooks,' he said in a quiet, emphatic tone.

Paul went to the doorway. 'Look, if they contained highly classified material, you honestly think I'd be so foolish as to hang on to them?'

Conran left the room and started slowly along the

147

passage. 'I've no very clear idea what political views you hold. But you've been keeping some rather odd company of late.' He looked briefly at Paul as they turned into the hallway. 'You had meetings at two public houses yesterday, the second with a man who is very well known to us. It simply won't do, Mr Marriott. You're causing us very serious concern.' He halted at the front door and put his hand on the latch.

'Why don't you just pick up Bernard Larke and have done with it?' Paul said angrily. 'Or is there someone at the Confederation for International Studies who'd prefer that you didn't?'

The other man looked at him, his narrow grey face suddenly bleak and cold. 'Don't tell me my business,' he said softly. 'We know what we're at. I'm only wondering if you do.' With that he opened the front door and went off down the stairs.

The little flat in which Paul found himself that evening looked as if it might be a safe house for some terrorist organisation. The living room had the shabby, neglected appearance of a furnished lodging: a two-month-old copy of *Time* magazine on a wooden table marked with cigarette burns; a gas fire equipped with a slot-meter; a fly-blown picture of Norwich Cathedral above the mantelpiece; faded green curtains drawn over the windows. He waited.

He had taken the most elaborate precautions coming here. A taxi to South Kensington Underground. Then four different trains, jumping from two of them just as the doors were closing. Finally, from Notting Hill Gate, he had taken the Central Line to Queensway. He had approached Chepstow House, Craven Square, circuitously and on foot by way of the back streets behind Bayswater Road. He felt certain that Conran's spooks hadn't followed him.

A man had let him into the flat, shown him to the

living room and promptly gone out through the front door. He wasn't alone though. He could hear two people talking in the next room.

It was a long time before they appeared, the door opening rather suddenly behind him. Gabriel came across the room followed by a woman. The woman had black hair and blue eyes; she was around thirty years of age, good-looking in a hard kind of way, plainly dressed in a blouse and skirt. She remained standing by the mantle-piece while Gabriel sat down.

There were no introductions, no preambles. Gabriel said, 'We want to make you a proposition.'

'Yes?'

'Suppose we were able to tell you what Larke had done to these two young people. You could use the information?'

Paul nodded.

'For a newspaper story?'

'That would depend. The material would have to be very carefully checked out. But one way or another I want to see the end of Larke and the Regiment of God.'

Gabriel smiled. 'Then our interests are identical. You tell us where Larke is, we'll give you – the material.'

'I don't know where he is,' Paul said.

'We don't believe you.' Gabriel turned to the woman. 'Do we, Molly?'

The woman took her hand off the mantlepiece and looked squarely at Paul. 'You told Gabriel that Bernard Larke's name had "come up" while you were talking to a fellow-reporter. You said the reporter might have "heard it mentioned" at one of the sect's meetings.' She shook her head. 'No, Mr Marriott. Larke's name would never have "come up", it would never have been "mentioned". You have to be lying. I think you've seen Larke. I think you know where he is.'

'You can think what you like,' Paul replied. 'But I can't go along with your proposition.'

'Why not?' Gabriel asked.

'I'm a journalist, not an informer,' Paul told him. 'I won't be a party to murder.'

'Always these muddled bourgeois loyalties,' Gabriel said impatiently. 'How can you want to protect a man like Larke?'

Paul shrugged. 'If you can nail him before I do, that's your business. But I'm not making any deals.'

'What if he nails you first?' Molly said. 'Or Trahearne does? Why not get yourself out of harm's way?'

Paul rose to his feet. He looked from the woman to Gabriel. 'Sorry. No dice,' he said.

Turning, he walked from the living froom, crossed the passage and went out through the front door.

Two short flights of stairs brought him to the ground floor. Passing an empty pram in the hall, he stepped out into the dark area surrounding Chepstow House.

He had just started for the gate when three men appeared. Swiftly and silently, they moved in on either side of him. He stopped, confronted by what looked like the front row of a rugger scrum. Dark against the lamp-light, solid as a wall, the men stood facing him for several seconds without speaking.

'Did you tell the lady what she wanted to know?' the man in the middle asked at length.

'I did,' Paul replied.

'Well, that's good. I'm pleased to hear that.'

There was another pause.

'Would you tell us again?' the man on the right said. 'Just to be sure.'

Paul didn't move or say anything. The door to the block was less than five paces behind him. They could crowd him against it in a matter of seconds. Whatever happened, he must move before they did.

'Where's Bernard Larke?' the man on the left asked.

'He's gone back to Armagh and taken Oliver Cromwell with him.' Even as Paul spoke, he threw himself to one side and kicked out wildly at the man on the right. He got him on the knee-cap just hard enough to make him lurch forward with a grunt of pain. The manoeuvre took him into the open. Useless to run for the gate. He spun round as the other two came at him. They were big men, but they were fast on their feet. Paul ducked and swung, chopping the first of them in the kidneys. The man gave a cry of pain and went down on his knees. But the other had got behind Paul; a crushing blow across the shoulders knocked the wind out of him and brought him to the ground. By now the first man had reappeared; with his good leg he gave Paul a vicious kick on the side of the head which sent him rolling over on his back. He had a blurred vision of the second man looming above him; he lashed out with both legs, caught his attacker in the pit of the stomach, then rolled over. As he did so, the man he had hit in the kidneys landed on him with both knees in the middle of his back. The other bent down and gave him a chop behind the ear.

The next thing he knew, he was on his feet. One man was holding his arms pinned behind him, another was in front of him, the third coming up to one side.

The man facing him took a step forward, lifted his fist and said, 'While you still have your teeth — where's Larke?'

'I don't know.' Paul could hardly get the words out. He was still half-dazed and could scarcely breathe.

The grip tightened on his arms. The man before him drew back his fist.

'Stop that! Let him go!' A woman's voice – Molly's – shouted suddenly from the doorway.

The fist remained poised for a moment in Paul's uncertain vision. Then it dropped. As the woman came towards them, the other man let go of his arms.

'You bloody idiots!' Molly pushed the man away from in front of Paul.

Paul didn't hesitate. He turned and ran, stumbling, through the gateway. As he started along the pavement, he heard Molly's voice in the yard. 'When the hell will you learn to obey orders? I told you to keep out of the way! You want to get your ugly faces in the newspapers, or what?'

He picked up a taxi in Bayswater Road. Fifteen minutes later he was climbing painfully up the stairway to his flat.

As he opened the front door, he heard the telephone ringing.

Switching on the lights, he entered the living room and picked up the receiver. 'Hello . . .'

'Paul . . .' a girl's voice said. 'Thank heavens I got you at last. I've been trying all evening.'

He stood leaning against the table. His whole body ached; his head was splitting and he felt sick and dizzy. He hadn't recognised the voice; he thought it might be Penny Armstrong, back from the Costa Brava, anxious to renew their affair.

'Who is it?' he asked.

'Nicola. . . . I'm calling from the convent, I've had a letter from that man you talked about – John Aubrey.'

'Yes?'

'He wants to sell me Rosamond's notebooks for twenty-five pounds.'

'What did he say?'

'I was to meet him tomorrow in Piccadilly, at six o'clock outside Swan & Edgar's. I'm going home for the weekend anyway, for – for the funeral. But I haven't got twenty-five pounds and I didn't know what to do.'

Paul thought a moment. The right thing was to call Conran; but he had no idea how to reach him. It would mean going through Trahearne. And he didn't want Trahearne getting to Aubrey before he did. Aubrey was at best an unreliable witness, possibly with a criminal record. There was no knowing what testimony he might give if Trahearne leaned on him. Nor was there any guarantee that the notebooks contained irrefutable evidence against Larke.

'Listen,' he said. 'I'll bring the money. I'll meet you there. Don't talk to anyone about this till you see me, understand?'

'Yes. . . . Has anything else happened?'

'One or two things. I'll tell you tomorrow.'

'All right. I'll be there. Good bye, Paul.'

Putting down the telephone, he went off to the bathroom to find some aspirins and clean up.

He made no attempt to cover his tracks as he drove to Newbury next day. If Conran's spooks wanted to follow him to Lady Beresford's country residence, they could do so. Crossing the Chiswick flyover on his way to M4, he punched the radio button under the dashboard.

> Love, love,
> I want someone to love.
> Someone to cry with,
> Live till I die with,
> Someone to love . . .'

Impatiently he switched off the radio. He only hoped the luncheon wouldn't be too protracted; he would have to allow two hours for the return journey if he were to reach Piccadilly in time to meet Nicola.

Leaving the motorway at the Newbury turn-off, he took the road to Lambourne as Diana Beresford had instructed. He found the house easily enough: a grey stone gateway with a porter's lodge and a drive leading to an ivy-covered Queen Anne mansion.

He pulled up just beyond the front door and got out. There were no other cars to be seen. Evidently he was the first to arrive. Crossing the driveway, he had started up the steps when he heard someone coming along a gravel path at the side of the house.

It was Diana Beresford. She came walking rather quickly towards him, her eyes on his face. He wondered why she wasn't smiling. A moment later two other figures appeared, following close behind her. General Stapleton and the Colonel.

The three of them were half a dozen yards away from Paul when a car swung into view from the other end of the house. It halted in front of him and two men climbed out. One of them was Bernard Larke. The other was Walter. Paul turned slowly and looked at Diana Beresford.

'I believe Mr Larke has things to say to you,' she informed him in a quiet and perfectly neutral voice.

He took a swift glance around It was all being done very subtly and very decorously. Colonel Ferris had his hand in his jacket pocket; the bulge there was a little too big for just his fist. As Walter moved forward, Paul caught no more than a glimpse of the sawn-off shotgun hanging from a leather sling at his shoulder. Walter stopped, opened the rear door of Paul's Triumph and stood waiting.

Then Larke came to the car and opened the driver's door. 'Get in, Mr Marriott,' he said.

Paul looked briefly at Diana Beresford. 'You're taking a big chance,' he said. 'Are you sure this is worth five million pounds?'

'Yes, I'm afraid it is.' Her eyes searched his face for a moment. 'If only you'd been more sensible. I feel sure we could have reached some compromise.'

'There's no compromising with the spiders,' he told her. 'Either you sweep them out of the corners or you pay the price of living with them.'

Turning away, he descended to the foot of the steps and paused. He could try to rush Walter; but there would also be Larke to contend with. And Ferris. The odds were hopelessly against him. Taking his keys from his pocket, he walked to the car and got in. Larke slammed the door after him, Walter hitting the back seat at the same moment.

'Drive,' Walter said. 'Do anything silly and I'll blow

your head off, I swear to God.'

They started forward, Larke's car following.

'Turn right,' Walter said suddenly.

They were still a long way from the gates. But just ahead was a track leading off the tree-lined driveway. Paul made the turn. The track wound through the trees, coming out near a paddock and a row of stable backs. In front of them was a gateway and the open countryside.

They passed through the gate. travelling now along a sandy track which cut across the deserted, undulating downland. A place evidently used for exercising race-horses.

Slowly and in silence they drove on over the wild landscape, Larke keeping a dozen yards behind. The weather was breaking, Paul noticed; huge leaden clouds piling up ominously to the north. A flock of birds rose at the sight of the cars and went flapping away into the distance.

> Black rooks
> Adorn
> The speechless fields.
> Like iron nails
> Their stillness
> Pins
> The living mind
> To horror
> Of the sky's indifference . . .'

Glancing in the mirror, he saw Walter's flat, cruelly expressionless eyes watching him from the back of the car.

They had travelled nearly three miles when the track ended, coming out on to a public laneway.

'Left,' Walter said.

They followed the lane for about two hundred yards. Paul thought they must be somewhere near the Hungerford road.

'Next gateway on the right,' Walter said.

Paul swung through the entrance. They were on a gravel drive, trees all round. Only when they came out of the wood did he realise that they were at the back of Greenfields.

They passed a vegetable garden, drove round a garage area and came to the front of the house. Paul stopped.

'Out,' Walter told him.

He climbed from the car. Walter was already standing with the gun levelled. He gestured to Paul and they moved to the steps.

Larke was going ahead of them. As he approached the front door it was opened by Robert, the other young man whom Paul had encountered on his first visit.

They all went inside. Robert closed the door. With Walter behind him, Paul followed Larke across the empty hall to the office.

They entered. Walter pushed the door to with his shoulder and took up a position a few feet from Paul. Paul glanced down at the gun. It was a 12-bore automatic with about six inches of barrel. The safety catch was off.

Larke turned around smartly and faced him. 'Walter has the first pressure on the trigger of that gun and it's not loaded for snipe,' he said quietly. 'You budge, he'll blast you. He'll have no alternative.'

'You go around kidnapping journalists, where do you think you'll finish up?' Paul said.

'Nobody's been kidnapped.' Larke continued to stand rigidly before him. 'You lunched with Lady Beresford today then went off for a weekend in the country.' He paused a moment, looking at the bruise on Paul's temple. Then he turned and moved behind the desk. 'Been in a scrap, have you?'

'Three men. I think they came from Armagh. They wanted to know where you were.'

'And you told them.'

'No,' Paul said. 'My newspaper doesn't pay me to get

people murdered.' He saw a faint look of puzzlement pass over Larke's face. 'But I've no doubt they'll run you to earth before very long.'

'Dirty, bloody Micks.'

'I couldn't agree with you more.'

Larke's moist, red lower lip stuck out aggressively. 'We're fifty strong here and the place is wired like Fort Knox. I'd even welcome a visit.' Leaning forward, he planted his fists on the desk-top. 'Now to business. Rosamond Clay. You met her in a Chelsea pub on Tuesday, 4 September. The following day she moved into your flat. After a while you began to find her difficult and demanding. You tried to get rid of her. She wouldn't go. On the morning of Wednesday the 12th there was a violent quarrel. You lost your temper and pushed her out of the window.'

'A likely story,' Paul said.

'You don't believe it now. But in a couple of days you will. You'll believe every blind word of it, I promise you.' Larke straightened up and put his hands behind his back. 'When you lunched with Lady Beresford today, you told her you'd had a visit from the police. You were worried. You were half-inclined to go to them and make a statement. You decided to think it over during the weekend.' The man paused, his bright bulging eyes looking straight into Paul's own. There was something almost hypnotic about the intensity of his gaze. 'On Monday you will telephone Chief Inspector Trahearne and make a confession. You will then put the confession down in writing and post it to him. After that you will take a suitcase containing some of Rosamond's possessions and go to Earls Court Mansions. You will leave the suitcase in the bedroom of your flat for the police to find. The next thing you will do is climb up on the roof. You will walk to the parapet. And you know what you'll do then?'

'I'll piss on you,' Paul said. 'That's what I'll do.'

'You throw yourself over. You won't be able to help

157

yourself. You'll *want* to do it.' Larke continued to stare fixedly at him for a moment. Paul had the disturbing impression that the man's eyes were made of hard, polished glass. 'We can't afford you, Mr Marriott. You've got in the way of something too important. The will of God.'

The silence in the room was broken by the sound of Walter clearing his throat. Larke turned and gestured to him. Walter backed across the room, opened the door and stepped into the hall. Coming round the desk, Larke motioned Paul ahead of him.

'Where are we going?' Paul asked.

'To the Music Room,' Larke told him.

They went along the hall, Larke leading, Walter bringing up the rear. Passing through a doorway at the back of the house, they descended a flight of stairs.

At the foot of the stairs was a passage. At the end of the passage, an open soundproof door. Paul could see little of what lay beyond. But as they approached, Robert emerged quickly from the room putting something into a canvas bag. They reached the door. Larke stood aside. At the same moment Paul received a violent blow in the back and went pitching forward. As he landed on his knees he heard the door slam behind him, the heavy latches being fastened.

Getting up from the floor, he looked around. The room measured about twelve feet by ten. The walls were bare and painted white. A single spotlamp equipped with a magnifying lens shone harshly from the ceiling above his head. There was no furniture of any kind. Only two stereo-speakers high up in the corners of one wall. Big speakers. At least a hundred watts, he thought. For several seconds he stood in the middle of the room, bewildered.

Then the music started. Wild, primitive rock rubbish. Only louder than he had ever heard it before. Sheer noise, pulverising, ear-splitting noise. An electric guitar stretching notes to tortured howls; the banging of a bass guitar; drums; a piano that someone seemed to be hitting with a ten-pound hammer. The great speakers big enough to hold it all, the music exploded and reverberated in the confined space, assaulting him like some elemental, physical force . . .

A poison is a substance which, when introduced into a living organism, causes the arrest or disruption of habitual processes upon which the functioning of that organism depends. Thus we destroy weeds, rats and harmful insects – by breaking down, distorting or confusing their internal chemistry. Poisons violate nature. They can defoliate forests, stop the respiratory systems in flies and the heartbeat of the largest mammal.

So too can the human brain, the electro-chemical theatre of the soul, be violated. With Mescaline, lysergic acid, psilocybine; as with other, more sophisticated hallucinogenic substances, the names of which are not to be found in any textbook . . .

Paul would later ask himself how the poison came to be introduced into his system. For the moment he had more urgent preoccupations.

Not least of these was the realisation that the music had not stopped, as at first he thought it had. The music had been turned into something else. The blasting rock rhythm had become silence – more, an orchestration of silences, of silences within silences passing over and through him like invisible shadows, perceived by some faculty he never knew he possessed. The realisation also came to him that he was lying on his back staring fixedly at the spotlight on the ceiling. Oddly passive, somehow dissociated from his own body, he let the waves of silence beat down on him. How long had the experience lasted? A minute? An hour? He had no way of knowing. Instinctively, as if to inquire of his mind what had occurred, he closed his eyes; just as a man in other circumstances would have opened them.

It had been going on in his head all the time. This was what he had been 'hearing'; what the music had become; these had been the waves passing through him. Only they were not just the abstract forms of waves. They had a terrible solidity, as durable and as indestructible as the cosmos. Irresistible, imperturbable, they flowed through his consciousness like some huge primeval tide. Mountainous waves; mountains and more monntains multiplying and multiplyirg. The limbs of massive giants stretching and stretching to infinity, inexhaustibly drawing silences out of silences out of silences. Vast explosions of silence out of monumental stillnesses within stillnesses within stillnesses, erupting and marching greyly, inexorably, patiently from Alpha to Omega and beyond – beyond the infinite to some Ultima Thule which was neither end nor beginning but another giant heaving and stretching into further and further infinities, a re-multiplication of a multiplicity of mountainous silences heaping themselves yet again endlessly and endlessly, colourelessly, prodigiously, and with a staggering lack of urgency, ever one upon the other.

Was this reality? Was this the real within the real, the kneading, infinitely slowly shaping, monstrously patient God-essence of all things?

As if in answer to his questions, another vision presented itself. A field of mouths. A plain rather, a plain stretching for ever made of mouths. The corners of the lips were moving as if, in some lunatic way, they still heard the music which Paul could not hear – but which he knew was in some unimaginable fashion informing and orchestrating the vision. The mouths should have been saying something but they weren't. Anything they said would have been irrelevant to the enormity of what was happening. The speechless fields? All at once the mouths vanished.

The stretching giants, the mountainous forces, were on the move again. Only now there was something hostile, malign about them. The edges of the dark, rolling shapes

160

had a sudden, terrifying lack of symmetry. A mind-shattering, panic-making irregularity of outline – the asymmetry of all asymmetry, the very form and essence of chaos, cruelly sharp, bewildering in their endless flux and change. He felt a sense of terror more profound than anything he had experienced in his worst nightmares, an unnameable threat striking at the very roots of his mind. . .

Someone was screaming. Screaming through the noise of the music. Larke was picking him up from the floor, Walter standing near by with the shotgun. The screams were his own. The moment he realised this, he stopped. For what seemed a very long time he stood in the middle of the room, half-supported by Larke. His teeth were chattering, his whole body shook as if he had been pulled from a tank of ice-cold water. As they led him away, he suddenly started to weep uncontrollably, assailed by some incomprehensible anguish.

He stumbled beside Larke across the hall and up two flights of stairs. The journey seemed to take a lifetime. He had a terrible sense of desolation, as if his mind had been pillaged, ransacked, stripped of everything familiar. He felt an almost overwhelming desire to start weeping again.

They pushed him into a room on the second floor. He staggered across it and half-fell on to a bed. Larke was standing in the doorway. 'Just a breather, Marriott,' he said. 'You'll be going down again shortly. After we've had another talk.' He smiled at Paul. 'A bit like drowning really. You see, it's only in the last session we stop the music.'

The door closed. A key turned in the lock.

For a long time Paul sat motionless on the bed, dully, confusedly trying to assess the damage that had been done to him. He was in pain. A pain that seemed to go right down through the centre of his brain like the cavity of a drawn tooth. When he made even the slightest movement he broke out in a sweat. He tried to still the panic that was churning inside him, the nameless indefinable dread

161

that seemed to be sending armies of ants crawling all over his scalp. He closed his eyes and almost instantly opened them again. For behind his eyes there lurked a naked terror, a raw panic too fearful to contemplate. He sat with his eyes wide open, sweating, shifting his gaze quickly from one object in the room to another. The room was deathly quiet. Not the faintest sound came from outside. The stillness, the absolute immobility of the ordinary things around him, became disturbingly oppressive. He longed to hear sounds – the ticking of a clock, voices, traffic. He had the feeling of being locked in a tomb.

Half an hour passed. An hour. The only movement was the slow changing of the sun's pattern on the floor. He was beginning to feel as if he were as immobile as the trappings of the room, the bed on which he sat, the chair, the ashtray on the table in front of him. He must think. 'A breather', Larke had said. Extraordinary how difficult he found it to relate one thought with another, to elaborate ideas even on the simplest level. He had to feel for his thoughts, gropingly, as you would feel for objects in a house that had been struck by lightning and plunged into darkness.

With an effort he got to his feet and crossed to the window. He tried to raise the sash, but it was locked. He could see the holes in the frame, recently made, for the Banham keys. He looked down. Nearly a thirty-foot drop to the ground. Even if he could jump, he would kill himself. He ran his hands over his face. If they put him back in the Music Room, he would kill himself anyway. He knew that now. He looked out of the window again, at the gravel path far beneath. It musn't happen to him. *It must not happen to him.* There was only Larke and Walter with the shotgun. Probably the rest of the youngsters in the house knew nothing of what was going on. He had been in tight situations before. Only then his mind had been whole, willing and commanding his body, sending the surge of adrenalin through his limbs; his mind the source of his strength, his quickness, his very will to survive – not a pit of horror behind his eyes.

The sunlight crept across the wall and vanished. He could see the sun now, low behind some tall trees on the far side of the grounds. He had been in the room nearly two hours.

Much later, when shadows were beginning to gather in the corners, he heard footsteps coming up the stairway. He got to his feet.

Larke reached the stairhead, Walter at his elbow. They had just started along the landing when they heard the shattering of glass from beyond the locked door. They ran the rest of the way. Larke turned the key and they burst into the room. The bottom of the window was completely smashed, only a few jagged edges of glass glinting in the last rays of the sun. Of Paul there was no sign.

The two men were half-way across the room, certain that they would see him lying on the gravel path below, when the legs of a chair hit Walter in the back like the horns of a charging bull. He dropped the gun and went sprawling. Larke turned and made a rush at Paul who had come from behind the door. Paul raised the chair and the man put up his hands to parry the blow; at the same moment Paul side-stepped, kicked him hard in the groin and brought the chair crashing down on his head. As Larke collapsed to his knees, Paul grabbed the shotgun from the floor and raced out.

He went pounding down the two flights of stairs. As he neared the hall, he heard Larke and Walter coming after him. He ran across the hall. 'This is our height and our home. Too high and too steep dwell we here for the unlean and their thirsts.' There were no young eagles to bar his path. Flinging open the front door, he dashed down the steps.

His car was where he had left it, a few paces from the entranceway. There was no sign of the other car. He pulled the driver's door open. Keys. He fumbled frantically in his pocket. Just then Larke and Walter appeared at the top of the steps. Paul turned and fired from the hip, the gun bucking in his hand. He saw the two men throw themselves behind the balustrade. In the seat now, he jammed the key into the lock and started the engine. Glimpsing Larke and Walter at the foot of the steps, he fired again. Then he dropped the gun, put the car into gear and drove off with the door still open. It slammed shut as he gathered speed, screeching and swaying erratically down the driveway towards the road.

He was shaking so violently he could hardly hold the wheel, mind and body protesting at the exorbitant demands he had made upon them. Heading towards Hungerford and the nearest entrance to the M4, he saw that there was no pursuit. Larke would have gained little by chasing him along the public highway. He didn't doubt, though, that a reception committee would be waiting for him at the other end.

Painfully he hauled the car round the slip road on to the motorway. Oddly, he felt no satisfaction at his escape; only the same emptiness, the same sense of isolation, of deep, indefinable panic. The effort he had made at the house had left him drained, shattered, almost totally spent. Sudden pains shot through his body and through his brain like violent electric shocks. Grimly he kept going, keeping to the inside lane, not daring to drive too fast.

Somehow he must hold himself together; he must think; he must plan. Useless to go to the police. A wild story about being kidnapped in the presence of three highly respectable members of the Establishment; drugged, poisoned, brainwashed by a God-crazy sergeant-major who believed that Friedrich Nietzsche was John the Baptist. What drug? What poison? The speechless fields. How could he begin to explain? To Trahearne of all people. No doubt Diana Beresford would testify that he had lunched at Woodlands and spent the afternoon there. His only hope was John Aubrey; Aubrey and perhaps the notebooks. But it was already after six; he had missed his appointment with Nicola. The car lurched and frantically he righted the wheel, pulling off the hard shoulder of the road. Steadying the car, he drove on into the storm-filled dusk.

By the time he reached Hesper Mews behind the block of flats it was almost dark. A cold wind struck him as he climbed exhaustedly from the driving seat. For a moment he stood leaning against the car trying to think what he was supposed to do. Frewin. That was it, he must call Arthur Frewin.

A few heavy drops of rain fell on him as he made his way along Bramham Gardens and round the corner to the Mansions.

Opening the street door, he paused and listened. There was no sound from the block; the lights in the well were out. He closed the door and moved on past the lift cage.

The word HELP daubed on the landing wall seemed to scream at him as he toiled up the stairway. Reaching the flat, he took his keys from his pocket. He was about to open the door when all at once he hesitated. He was sweating again; his knees were shaking and his teeth had started to chatter. It took him several seconds to understand. He was afraid to open the door. He was afraid to go inside. Some deep, irrational dread held him back. What was it? He thought of the long, shadow-filled passages beyond the door, the empty rooms, the open windows. The scullery. Yes, that was it. The scullery. He couldn't rid himself of the idea that Fred was back; an invisible presence waiting for him at the other end of the flat. He had never been afraid of the ghost before. Now the thought that it might be lurking in the half-darkness beyond the kitchen filled him with an unholy terror. In the Music Room, for a moment, he thought he had glimpsed something profound and horrifying – the vision of a blind immaterial force, a demiurge, moving mindlessly and mysteriously between measureless infinities. . . . It was his terror of the irrational that held him back now; the idea of Fred's chill, lonely, random, immaterial existence in the little back room. He stood helplessly, clutching the key in his hand. If God were anything at all, he thought dully, then he must be an illusionist. The danger, the deadly danger, lay in seeing the Illusionist at work.

Somewhere a door was swinging and banging in the wind. Only gradually did he become conscious of the sound. Turning, he looked upward. The door to the attic.

He didn't quite know why he started up the stairs; perhaps out of some obscure compulsion; perhaps only to delay the moment when he must enter the flat.

The attic was in darkness, the door to the roof open beyond. Ducking under the beams, he went to the door and stepped out on to the fire-walk. There was nobody to be seen, the wind howling in the television aerials above his head, bumping against the chimney pots. He moved to the parapet and looked down into the dark area, at the flight of steps leading from the porter's flat where Rosamond had lain. The parapet was only knee-high. Gripping the edge, he leaned out a little further. He only had to let go and he would topple headlong into the void.

'Paul!'

He straightened and turned. A figure was hurrying towards him from the shadow of one of the chimneys, a figure in jeans and a T-shirt. For a wild moment he thought it was Rosamond. A hand took hold of his arm and pulled him away from the parapet. A moment later he was stumbling back into the attic.

'What happened? What were you doing out there?' Nicola was staring at him in a bewildered fashion. 'I heard someone coming. I didn't know who it was.'

'Piccadilly,' he said. 'You went to Piccadilly.'

'Of course. I met John Aubrey. We waited for ages, but you didn't turn up. I came here looking for you. Where have you been?'

'The Music Room.'

'What?' She took him by the shoulders and turned him towards the dim light of the doorway. 'You've been hurt. You look terrible. . . .'

'Greenfields,' he said. 'In Berkshire. Where Rosamond was. I got away.' He put his hands up to his face for a moment, trying to collect his thoughts. He couldn't cope with events, he realised, if they moved too quickly. He mustn't be pushed. For a long time he just stood holding his head. Then he took his hands away and met Nicola's frightened gaze. 'You didn't get the notebooks, then?'

She shook her head. 'I only had five pounds. I gave him that. For an address. The doctor's . . .'

'Wait. We'll talk downstairs,' he told her.

Taking her hand, he led her across the attic and down to the landing. He got his keys out again and unlocked the front door. Holding her hand more tightly, he entered the hall.

The wind, carrying flurries of rain, was blowing through the open window of the study. He crossed the room, closed the window then came back and switched on the desk light. 'What doctor?' he asked.

'The one in Wimpole Street. His name's Drummond. Eighty-four Wimpole Street.'

'Drummond?'

'Yes. It must be the doctor Rosamond was supposed to be seeing. The one Aubrey heard Gail Canning talk about.'

'Where did Aubrey get this from?'

'He said it was in the flyleaf of one of the notebooks. He said I could have them anytime, but I've got to bring the money myself.'

Paul stood, trying hard to think. The he turned to her

167

quickly. 'Come on,' he said.

'Where are we going?'

'Wimpole Street.'

Leaving the room, he led her down the passage to the hall again. He opened the front door and they went out onto the landing. Just then the stairwell lights came on and they heard the street door slam. He pulled her back inside and closed the door. Footsteps were coming up the stairs. His arm round her shoulder, they retreated a little way down the hall.

The footsteps reached the landing and halted. Two shadowy outlines appeared against the glass panel of the door. The bell rang, loud-sounding in the silence of the flat. There was a long pause. The bell rang again. The two figures held a muttered consultation outside. Then they turned and went back down the stairs.

Paul moved to the living room. While Nicola stood watching him from the passage, he crossed to the window. Standing behind one of the curtains, he looked down. He saw the two men emerge from the block and go across the street. There they stopped and stood side by side on the pavement, watching the entrance. In the darkness and rain he couldn't be sure, but he thought one of them must be Walter.

For a long time he stood by the curtain. The rain had grown heavier, the wind gusting down the street, people in their summer clothes running with their heads bent against the storm. The two men remained motionless, their eyes fixed on the entranceway of the building.

Suddenly the telephone shrilled behind Paul. The sound made him start, sent a trickle of sweat running down the back of his neck. He edged cautiously away from the window and picked up the receiver. 'Yes?'

'Paul, this is David.' Plummer sounded irritable. 'About that copy of yours . . .'

'What copy?'

There was a little silence at the other end. 'The rabies

168

story,' Plummer said almost menacingly. 'Merlin expects to see it on page three tonight. I need two thousand words from you.'

With a great effort, Paul brought his mind to bear. The rabies story: some notes on his desk; a string of ideas which had once been in his head but which were now no longer there.

'Paul. . . . Are you listening to me? What's the matter?'

'I got bitten by that mad dog,' Paul told him. 'The one in Berkshire.'

'You got what—?'

The two men on the pavement seemed to be talking earnestly together; then they both looked up and down the street. Perhaps they were expecting others.

'I'll phone it through to you,' Paul said.

'Oh, Christ. All right. I'll put you on—'

'No, I can't do it now. I've got to go and see a doctor.'

He put down the telephone. For several seconds he didn't move, his eyes on the pavement below. Then all at once he turned and went back across the room.

'Who are they?' Nicola asked. She looked very small and scared standing in the long, dark passage.

He didn't answer, going past her to the study. Searching about on his desk, he found a small piece of perforated plastic, the kind of thing you use when correcting typescripts. He put it in his pocket and came out of the room again.

'Is there no one you can go to?' Nicola asked. 'The police?'

'No one,' he said. Taking her by the arm, he led her back to the front door. 'At this moment I don't think I've a friend in the world.'

They slipped quickly out on to the landing. He kept his hand on her arm as they hurried down the stairs to the ground floor.

Going to the door of the porter's flat, he took out the piece of plastic and inserted it into the jamb. It was a trick that had been used by generations of burglars. He simply pushed the plastic against the latch of the Yale lock and forced it inwards. The door opened.

It was almost pitch dark in the little flat. They groped their way across two empty rooms, the air hot and stale. In the kitchen, he fumbled with the bolts of the back door. The moment he turned the handle it crashed open in the wind. They climbed the steps and crossed the area to the gate.

Her hand held tightly in his, they ran through the drenching rain along Bramham Gardens and up the deserted mews. Like Theseus in the labyrinth, he thought, hunting the Minotaur; Nicola his Ariadne.

They climbed into the car and he started the engine. Turning across the mews and grinding the front bumper against the far wall, he backed up and headed for Collingham Gardens.

As they drove along Cromwell Road and Knightsbridge, he tried to tell her what had happend; Diana Beresford's luncheon invitation; Larke and the Music Room; why it was he daren't go to the police.

What seemed like several hours later he pulled up in front of the house in Wimpole Street and made his way a little unsteadily across the pavement. He pressed the bell marked 'Dr Drummond' and waited, Nicola standing close beside him and shivering in the rain.

The door was opened by an elderly woman wearing a hat and raincoat. She was about to speak when Paul pushed Nicola ahead of him into the hall.

'Do you have an appointment?' the woman asked, looking slightly startled. 'It's after hours . . .'

'This is an emergency,' Paul said. 'I have to see Dr Drummond. Tell him it's about Rosamond Clay.'

'Well, I don't know. . . . If you'll come in here a moment.' She led them to a waiting room. 'What name is it?' she asked.

'Marriott. Paul Marriott.'

The woman nodded and went off along the hall towards a flight of stairs.

Paul and Nicola stood together in the silent, elegantly furnished room.

'I should have sent you home,' he said.

She shook her head. There were little drops of rain on her face; her wet T-shirt clung to her slim body. Her eyes, big and anxious, looked steadily at him.

'You shouldn't be here,' he said wearily. He wasn't Theseus in the labyrinth, he told himself; he was a sleep-walker in an impenetrable jungle filled with murderous animals. Why the hell hadn't he called Frewin?

'I *am* here.' She came to him suddenly and put her hands on his shoulders. 'Don't tell me you haven't got a friend in the world. You've got me.' She looked up at him. 'Besides, I'm safer with you than with anyone.'

'No, listen . . . you'd better make a run for it. For all we know, Bernard Larke could be upstairs with the doctor.'

'He could be out in the street,' she said. 'Or one of them could be waiting for me at home.'

He stood holding her a moment. The way she said it, it seemed to make sense. He wasn't thinking clearly enough to be sure.

Then the door opened and the woman appeared. She gave Paul an unfriendly look and said, 'The doctor will see you now.'

Paul went out of the room with her. She closed the door and said, 'The room straight in front of you at the head of the stairs.'

He nodded and went along the hall. He always seemed to be climbing stairs. At the top, across a landing, the door to the doctor's consulting room stood ajar. He opened it and went in.

Dr Drummond was a big man, about six foot two and broad in proportion. He had a round, red-veined face and a large brown moustache; his eyes were also brown, small

171

and rather bloodshot. Rising from behind his desk as Paul entered, he said, 'Good evening. Mr Marriott, is it? Won't you please sit down?'

Paul came and sat in front of the desk. The doctor resumed his position in the chair. 'Mrs Nesbitt tells me you've come to inquire about one of my patients,' he said.

'Rosamond Clay,' Paul replied.

'Clay?' The doctor frowned and shook his head. 'A private patient?'

'Very much so.'

Drummond sat back, looking oddly at his visitor. .I'm quite certain I'm not treating anybody called Clay. In any case, you understand I can't discuss patients' affairs with strangers.'

'Rosamond Clay committed suicide just over a week ago,' Paul said. 'I'm covering the story for my newspaper.'

The doctor continued to regard him, searchingly and perplexedly. Then he leaned forward, putting his elbows on the desk. 'Look, my name's Peter Drummond. I'm a psychiatrist. Are you sure you've come to the right place?'

'I know your name's Drummond. I thought you might be a psychiatrist. And yes, I have come to the right place.'

'Then perhaps you'd be so good as to explain.'

'It's no use,' Paul said. 'You've been blown. I've got Rosamond Clay's notebooks.'

'I beg your pardon?'

'The notebooks. The ones she put everything down in. I bought them this evening from John Aubrey. If you don't know who he is, you can ask Gail Canning.'

There was a brief silence. 'I'm terribly sorry,' Dr Drummond said, 'but I'm afraid I haven't the faintest idea what you're talking about.'

'The little thing you and Larke have been running together.'

'And who might he be?' The doctor's tone had become softer.

'Your partner at Greenfields. The Eagles' Nest. Let's stop playing around, shall we? I spent the afternoon there. I've been in the Music Room.'

'The Music Room?'

'Where they turn music into mountains.'

'How remarkable.' Dr Drummond ran the back of his hand over his moustache. 'Truly remarkable.'

'Your psychoannihilation technique – the one that killed Rosamond Clay and Jack Tendler.'

The other nodded; there was a deeply preoccupied expression on his face. 'I'd like to get this perfectly clear,' he said in an almost soothing voice. 'You were at a place called the Eagles' Nest, in the Music Room, where certain phenomena took place.'

'Only I escaped,' Paul told him. 'I thought the news might have got to you.'

The doctor leaned back, tapping his fingers gently on the desk. 'Not as yet,' he said.

Paul sat a moment. The doctor's little bloodshot eyes remained impenetrable, scrutinising him as if he were a biological specimen on a slab. He knew how odd he must look: his rain-soaked clothes, his bruised forehead, the sweat standing out on his face. He had to grip the arms of the chair to keep himself from shaking. He felt that he had almost reached the end of his resources. Another minute and he would collapse.

'This man Larke,' Drummon said. 'Would he be a doctor by any chance?'

'No, he's a parachutist. You know that bloody well.'

'Yes, of course.' With a little exhalation of breath, the doctor leaned forward again. 'So what am I supposed to do?'

'Give yourself up to the police. Tell them how you caused the deaths of Rosamond Clay and the Tendler boy. If you turn Queen's Evidence against Larke and the Regiment of God, you may get off lightly. I'm giving you a chance.'

'Very good of you.' Drummond picked up a pencil, fiddled with it and put it down again. 'One thing. I'm a little unclear what brought you here in the first place. Why did you come to me particularly?'

'Because it's all in the notebooks,' Paul said. 'Your name and address, every detail of what happened. I told you. You've been blown.'

'Yes, I see,' Drummond said quickly. 'I'd forgotten about the notebooks.' He picked up the pencil once more and stared at it. 'So I'm to give myself up to the police, turn Queen's Evidence and confess to a double murder. And you're going to put it all in your newspaper.'

Paul nodded.

The doctor laid the pencil aside and folded his hands. 'My housekeeper tells me you came here with a young woman.'

'Yes.'

'A relative?'

'A friend.'

'A friend. I see.' The man got to his feet and came round the desk. 'I think I'd better have a word with her, if you don't mind.' He started across the room.

Paul turned to protest. But all at once he realised he could do no more. He had simply run out of steam. A feeling of utter helplessness, of impotence, had come over him; the pains were shooting through his body again; every time he closed his teeth he seemed to feel a violent electric shock. He was overwhelmed by a crushing sense of exhaustion, an urgent and almost irrepressible desire to sleep.

'You just wait there and try to relax, Mr Marriott,' the doctor said from the doorway. 'I won't be long.' He went out, closing the door behind him.

For a minute or two Paul sat without moving. Suppose Drummond were perfectly innocent? What if Aubrey had sold Nicola a false bill of goods, simply picked a name out of the telephone directory? It wasn't too improbable. A drug addict who would do anything for a fiver. He pulled himself out of the chair. Next thing, he would be locked in the psychiatric ward of some hospital with nothing to look forward to but a visit from Trahearne.

He crossed the room, pulled open the door and stepped out on to the landing.

What happened during the next minute had all the appearances of being stage-managed: one of those melodramatic moments so timed by chance as to have the precision of a neatly contrived theatrical performance.

A clock started to chime in a room across the landing. As Paul turned his head, a woman in a white overall appeared in the doorway. Two more chimes of the clock and he recognised her. Gail Canning from the discotheque.

On the next chime, the front doorbell rang. The woman in the hat and coat went down the hall. The chimes ceased at exactly the instant she opened the door. Stepping back, she gave a slightly comical, quavering little screech. The only false note in the scene.

A man was already coming past her up the hall. A man in a black jersey, a nylon stocking over his head, a gun in his hand.

Dr Drummond emerged from the waiting room and stopped as if he had walked into a brick wall. The man halted, too. He stood with his legs apart and his knees bent, raising a massive, long-barrelled revolver in both hands. For a moment the two figures remained frozen. Then the gun went off, an ear-splitting explosion in the confined space. Paul heard Nicola scream. Drummond had gone crashing back against the door-frame; a thing with only half a head, he was sliding limply to the floor. By the time he came to rest, the gunman was half-way down the steps.

Paul raced for the hallway. With the feeling of a man who had been caught up in some hideous nightmare, he grabbed hold of Nicola and together they fled from the house.

A car went roaring by along the street as he climbed into the Triumph, the girl beside him. Crashing the gears and swerving perilously, he drove off into the rain. At the first interesection they nearly came to grief, shooting through some red lights and narrowly escaping a collision.

'Where are we going now?' Nicola asked.

'My doctor.'

She gave him a look. 'It's about time,' she said.

The drive to Redcliffe Square was one he would remember for the rest of his life. It took him more than half an hour. By the time he parked the car, front wheels well up on the pavement before Chris's house, he knew that he couldn't have gone another yard.

Nicola helped him from the car, across the pavement and up the steps. He rang the bell. The automatic lock buzzed and he saw Chris coming down the hall.

'What's happened here?' the doctor asked as they entered the study. He was looking with understandable curiosity at Nicola.

Paul sank into a chair and put his head in his hands. 'You tell him,' he said to her.

It was surprising how much she had been able to gather of the events at Greenfields from the somewhat garbled account he had given her in the car. She told Chris Maitland the whole story, quickly and concisely, from her meeting with Aubrey in Piccadilly to the shooting of Dr Drummond. Listening to her, Paul felt a certain astonishment. His admiration for Nicola was growing by the minute. Walking out of a convent school into the horror of the evening's happenings, she had never wavered or panicked; not for a single moment had she lost her self-possession. She was beyond doubt a very remarkable young creature.

Whe she had finished, Chris stood looking down at Paul for a moment. 'Obviously some kind of hallucinogen,' he said. 'Can you tell me how you feel?'

Haltingly and with difficulty, Paul described

176

his symptoms.

Chris nodded slowly. 'To put it as simply as possible, hallucinogenic drugs affect that part of the brain which handles its own programming,' he explained. 'You have a bad trip, accidentally or deliberately brought about, and the programming mechanism goes seriously off-beam. You become de-motivated.'

'I feel de-motivated,' Paul said.

'What you appear to be suffering from are the symptoms of an acute depression. . . . Tell me, what do you have to do? Find this man Aubrey?'

'Find Aubrey, yes. He has to give up those notebooks.' Paul sat back helplessly. 'I'm supposed to turn in some copy tonight. So I could lose my job. Or I could be arrested for murder or shot by a gang of Irishmen.'

'You really are a marvel.' Chris shook his head. Then he crossed the room and opened the door. 'I'm going to mix you a cocktail,' he said. 'I call it my "Wernher von Braun." It'll send you up like the proverbial rocket. You'll feel very chirpy indeed for about three hours. I hope not too chirpy. After that you'll go out like a light. You'll sleep the clock round. I'm sorry, but three hours is all I can give you. Any more, I might be doing you harm.'

He went out of the room. There were sounds of bottles being opened, something being stirred. A few minutes later he reappeared carrying a glass of some cloudy-looking liquid and a small phial of pills.

'Drink it down,' he said, coming over to Paul. 'And for goodness sake call me tomorrow.'

Paul swallowed the concoction. It tasted vile.

'No stimulants, no alcohol,' Chris told him. 'You're going to feel pretty high. Also your judgement and co-ordination will be affected, so better not drive your car. If you find yourself getting over-excited, take two of these pills.'

Paul put the phial in his pocket. They all waited. After

about ten minutes the 'Wernher von Braun' began to work. He felt it in the back of his neck first, somewhere near the base of his skull: a tightening, a stirring at the roots of his nervous system; he found he could close his teeth without their feeling like lumps of electrically charged cotton wool. More gradually, still emanating from his brain stem, a warm glow, a sense of exhilaration, began to suffuse itself through his body. He felt suddenly whole again, miraculously put back in touch with some deep inner source of strength and illumination from which he had been cut off during the past hours. The potion was well-named. It was like coming round from the dark side of the moon. He got to his feet.

'Better?' Chris asked.

'Much better.' He crossed the room, taking Arthur Frewin's telephone number from his pocket. Picking up the receiver, he dialled.

Mrs Frewin answered. 'Oh, Mr Marriott. . . . My husband called about ten minutes ago and left a message for you. I wrote it down. Just a minute.'

There was a pause. He could picture the woman searching for a piece of paper in the chaos of the garden room. The sound of the children's voices came faintly over the line. 'Is it Daddy? Is it Daddy?'

'No, it isn't Daddy. Run along to bed now. . . . Here it is,' she said to Paul. 'He wanted you to know he'd found out where John Aubrey was living. Sixteen Maple Place, off Goldhawk Road near Shepherd's Bush Green. He was on his way there when he phoned. He said you'd understand.'

'Yes. Thank you, Mrs Frewin.' Paul put down the telephone. 'I'm going to need a taxi,' he said.

'You won't get one on a night like this,' Chris told him. He came to the telephone. 'I'll try my car-hire firm. It's only round the corner. They're usually pretty good.' He made the call then turned round. 'There'll be a car here in a moment,' he said. 'Who's Frewin?'

178

'A private detective.' Paul looked troubled. 'Aubrey doesn't know him. I only hope Frewin doesn't scare him away. . . .'

The fear was still nagging at his mind as he sat with Nicola in the back of the car. If Aubrey disappeared, it might take the rest of the night to find him. And he only had three hours.

'Don't worry,' Nicola said, as if discerning his thoughts. 'He'll be there. But you must let me talk to him. I'm sure he meant it when he said he wouldn't deal with anybody but me.'

Paul sat back, frowning. 'I wonder why, though?'

The car slowed as it turned off Goldhawk Road into Maple Place. 'Sure this is what you want, guv?' the driver asked.

Paul looked out through the rain. There wasn't a light to be seen anywhere. Most of the ground-floor windows were covered with sheets of corrugated iron, boards nailed across the doors. 'Yes,' he said. 'Number sixteen.'

The car pulled up outside the house. 'Will you wait?' Paul asked.

'Well, it doesn't look as if you'll be long, does it?' the driver said.

Paul got out of the car with Nicola and they climbed the steps. The door was open a few inches. He gave it a push and it swung inwards creakily.

The only light came from a window at the back of the house, the glow of a lamp in the neighbouring street. Signs here and there that the place had been occupied by squatters: refuse-filled carrier bags and empty milk bottles on the floor; a stub of candle stuck on the newel post at the foot of the stairs. The house was completely silent; only the racket of the storm outside; water dripping somewhere through the leaking roof. Evidently the squatter colony had moved on. But where was Aubrey? With a growing sense of disquiet, Paul led Nicola along the hall. A few bottles went rolling noisily across the

179

floorboards as they approached the back room. If there had been anybody about, they would have shown themselves by now. It was only too clear that Frewin must have come and gone.

He entered the room. The window was half-open at the top, hanging askew on a broken sash cord, the rain pouring in. He had taken a few paces when his foot struck something on the ground; something soft and solid. He felt Nicola grab hold of his arm. They both stood, straining their eyes down into the darkness.

The noise of footsteps came so suddenly that he scarcely had time to think. They sounded like thunder on the bare treads of the stairs. Two men coming down fast. He pushed Nicola behind the door and heard her give a stifled gasp of terror. There was no possible escape. He thought of the two men at Earl's Court, the figures he had seen on the pavement; one of them almost certainly Walter.

The pair reached the hall. An explosion of light as a torchbeam hit the doorway.

It was then Paul saw Aubrey. Aubrey lying face down on the floor, his face in a pool of blood. Frewin was staring at him from the opposite side of the room, his mouth hanging open in an expression of blank astonishment. He was sitting on the floor with his shoulders propped against the wall, a commando knife with a knuckleduster handle stuck in his heart.

Then the two men came crowding through the door and the torch glared in Paul's face.

'You seem to have started a minor war, Mr Marriott,' a voice said.

The beam dropped and Paul recognised Victor Conran.

'Who's this?' Conran asked, nodding towards Nicola.

Paul told him.

'A bit young for this kind of thing, aren't you?' Conran turned from the girl to look disapprovingly at Paul.

Nicola stood, small and bedraggled, before them; she was trembling slightly and her eyes were wide with shock.

'I wanted to help,' she whispered. 'They murdered my sister. They did – something terrible to her. . . . It was all in the notebooks. We. . . .'

'All right, Miss Clay,' Conran said. He glanced at the man beside him. 'Take her to the car and wait for us, will you?'

'Yes, sir.' The man led Nicola from the room and out through the back door.

'We've called the police,' Conran said to Paul. 'They'll be here in a few minutes.'

Paul looked across at the grotesque figure propped against the wall. 'A man called Arthur Frewin,' he said.

'Yes. He'd been keeping in touch with us since Ballard hired him,' Conran replied. 'It was he told us Aubrey might be here. Unfortunately we arrived too late. A couple of men were searching the room. They scarpered when we came in.'

'Who were they?'

'Probably Bernard Larke and one of his boys.' There was a chair in the corner and Conran went and laid his torch on it. His lean face looked gaunt and weary in the up-slanting light. 'They must have been looking for the notebooks. We found them under a floorboard.' He put his hand in his overcoat pocket and pulled out two slim green-covered books.

Paul frowned. 'How could Larke possibly have known the books existed?' he asked.

'A good question.' The security man opened one of the books and glanced at the flyleaf. 'Rosamond Clay must have visited Dr Drummond on at least one or two occasions. In her state of mind, it's possible she let something slip.'

Paul nodded. It made some sense. Gail Canning would have known that Aubrey had been Rosamond's only constant companion during the weeks after she left Greenfields. If she had given the books to anybody for safe keeping, it must have been him.

Conran was holding out the book. There was an expression on his face that puzzled Paul. Coming over, he took it from him. Dr Drummond's address was on the flyleaf as Aubrey had said. He turned to the rest, feeling a sudden shock as he did so. There was nothing but pages of wildly scrawled, partially indecipherable words: sometimes the same word written over and over again like 'threshold, threshold, threshold' covering a whole page. Parts of words, broken syllables; here and there just line after line of sharply pointed wave patterns. It gave him an immediate and vivid picture of what she had become; the tortured wreckage of her mind. He shoved the book back at Conran and looked at the two dead men on the floor. Perhaps it was the effect of Chris's potion, but he felt a macabre, almost irresistible desire to burst out laughing. Rosamond, in her deluded state, must have thought the two books contained vital information. The only articulate writings had been contained in the book she had left in the attic, the one she considered least important. He understood now why John Aubrey had insisted on selling the books to no one but Nicola. He must have known all along that they were worthless and had hoped to make an easy touch.

He turned back to Conran. 'Dr Drummond was murdered this evening,' he said.

'Yes, we know. We had a police flash about twenty minutes ago. There's a manhunt on for Liam O'Connor. We'll have him in a couple of hours.'

'Liam O'Connor?'

'One of the Young Turks from Ulster. His brother was killed by the security forces last month and he came over here on a campaign of vengance. . . .'

'Starting with Gerald McDermot in Hampstead last week.'

'Gerald McDermot of the Confederation for International Studies, yes. He'd worked in Ulster. He'd been a marked man for some time. Then you went to Gabriel and talked to him about Larke. Larke was an obvious target for O'Connor. He and his men picked up Skeggs in Coptic Street this evening. They worked him over and among other things must have got Drummond's address.' Moving away from the corner, Conran forestalled Paul's next question. 'Dr Drummond had been an army psychiatrist. He worked at the same interrogation centre as Larke in Armagh and was one of the few people who opposed Larke's dismissal. Later he resigned from the Services himself, principally because he believed the authorities weren't being tough enough on terrorist prisoners.'

'A bit unusual for a psychiatrist,' Paul said.

'Not necessarily. He'd served in Malaya and Korea. He'd made a special study of communist interrogation methods. Knowing what he did, I don't think his attitude was entirely unjustified.'

'He was a bit bent, though?'

. The other man made no comment. He turned, his shadow spreading huge across the ceiling, and came back down the room.

'What was going on between Larke and Drummond?' Paul asked. 'Am I allowed to know?'

Conran considered a moment. 'I can tell you a little. If only to stop you and your newspaper from indulging in irresponsible speculation.' He gave a faint smile. 'I'm going to put on the hook, Mr Marriott. This is under the Official Secrets Act. There can be no question of your repeating or printing a word of it.' He stood a moment, his back to the chair. 'There's a science you may never have heard of called psycho-technology. I stress, an unprintable term. It was coined by the CIA, who have spent the past twenty years and hundreds of millions of dollars looking for a drug that would change the human personality; enable them to to "rewrite a man's psychic scenario" in their own jargon. A drug that would make a prisoner instantly amenable to interrogation; with which

183

a person could be "re-programmed" to perform any desired task. The philosopher's stone of the intelligence world. Perhaps the ultimate weapon in the hands of one side or the other. Unfortunately, in spite of all their efforts, the Americans have got absolutely nowhere in their researches. The Russians, on the other hand, have been a little more successful.' Conran paused, a dark figure against the garishly lit corner. 'To understand Larke, we have to go back to General Anderton. While General Anderton was a prisoner in Vietnam, he met several American officers who had been subjected to an astonishingly powerful form of brainwashing. Those of them who survived long enough to be repatriated are now living under close surveillance in psychiatric hospitals, not because they're dedicated communists – which they are – but because they're suicidal. All of them are suffering from the effects of a drug we'll call "X". A hallucinogen like Mescaline or LSD, only vastly more potent. Again like LSD, a substance which is extremely easy to manufacture and which need only be administered in very small quantities. We know the KGB have been researching "X" for years. The Americans have the formula, but for moral reasons they've been unable to experiment with it even on volunteers. Effective as it is, the substance still doesn't work perfectly. Although the victims finish up believing everything they've been told to believe, they're left with an overwhelming urge to destroy themselves. Now, Anderton learned all about the drug while he was being debriefed by US intelligence officers. He must have discussed the subject with Larke, who in turn talked to Drummond. Larke had also attended courses at the Chemical Warfare Establishment where lectures on psycho-technology are part of the curriculum.'

'He and Drummond decided to experiment with the drug,' Paul said quietly, 'using some of the kids at Greenfields.'

'I know it sounds incredible. But remember, no one has

184

ever been able to test the drug properly in the West. For all we know, the Soviets may have perfected it by now. Larke thought that if he could succeed, it would put a weapon of unparalled power into the hands of the Regiment of God.'

'All right. Larke is more than a little mad and Drummond is some kind of fanatic. But why did they let Rosamond Clay and Jack Tendler loose in London after they'd been given the treatment?'

'We can't be sure. Perhaps Larke panicked. The youngsters were hopelessly psychotic and suicidal. He couldn't keep them at Greenfields for ever. The only alternative was to murder them, which would have been equally risky.' Conran moved past Paul and stood in the doorway. They could both hear the sound of cars coming up the street. 'He may have thought they'd take their lives much sooner than they did. In any case they were too far gone to give evidence against him. And we believe the idea had been firmly planted in their minds that the last thing they must do was go back to their homes. Then there was Drummond. As a highly respectable psychiatrist he could always testify that they were suffering from the effects of a bad trip on LSD or some similar drug. It was only unfortunate that one of them happened to fall to her death past a crime reporter's window.'

The cars were pulling up outside, doors opening and slamming.

'But what have you been doing all the time?' Paul asked. 'You could have pulled Larke in.'

'We're not living in a police state, Mr Marriott. The drug can be administered from an ordinary aerosol spray. It dissipates within minutes, leaving absolutely no trace. We hadn't a shred of evidence.'

'Then I'll give you some,' Paul said. 'Your demented psychotechnologist had me in his laboratory this afternoon.'

'What?' Conran stood staring at him. Men were

185

coming in through the front door now, torches flashing, footsteps loud on the floorboards.

'I was going round under the influence of Brand X until I saw my doctor half an hour ago.'

Conran continued to stare at him, for a moment ignoring the policemen who were crowding the hall at his back.

'I thought you were having me followed,' Paul said.

'We've never had you followed,' Conran replied. 'We knew you'd been dealing with Gabriel because we were informed of the fact.'

Paul had no time to ask who had done the informing. Conran had turned and was talking to a couple of plain-clothes men in the doorway. They conferred for several minutes, then Conran looked back at Paul and said, 'You can tell me about this in the car.'

'Is that your driver waiting outside, sir?' one of the policemen asked.

'Tell him he can go home,' said Paul. 'I'll settle the bill in the morning.'

He followed Conran from the room, along a passage and out through the back door. Making their way along a rubbish-filled alley, they came to the next street.

The man who had been with Conran in the house climbed from the back of a grey Rover 3500. Paul got in beside Nicola, Conran and the other after him. There were two men in the front: a driver and a radio operator.

As Conran sat down, the operator turned and said. 'Message from Periscope Three, sir. Rolls Bentley ARJ607D left Belgrave Square five minutes ago. Bernard Larke driving. Passengers – General Stapleton, Colonel Farris, Lady Beresford and Antonia Unwin. Heading west.'

'Periscope Three following?' Conran asked.

'Discreetly, sir'.

Paul looked round at Conran. 'If you believe what I've just told you, you can have them arrested, surely? Manslaughter and conspiracy to defraud.'

'I do believe you and I'm going to have them taken in for questioning,' Conran said ungraciously. 'Get me Information Room,' he told the radio operator.

The man hadn't moved, his body twisted awkwardly as he continued to look over the back of the seat. 'There was another message, sir. As Periscope Three pulled away, they report they had a visual from Beefeater.'

'A visual from Beefeater?' Conran leaned forward. For a moment he sat frowning, his elbows on his knees. 'Belgrave Square, driver,' he said. 'Quickly.'

The car pulled out from the kerb headed down the street.

'What about the call to Information Room, sir?' the radio operator asked.

'Hold it,' Conran said.

Paul turned to Nicola; she gave him a brief, tense little smile; he squeezed her hand and was surprised how cold it felt. With a screech of tyres they swung into Goldhawk Road. The name Beefeater meant nothing to him. Nor could he understand why the mysterious 'visual' should have delayed the arrest of Larke and his companions. One thing he did know: if Antonia Unwin were going to the country with Stapleton and Ferris, it could only be to sign away her fortune to the Regiment of God; a transaction that was due to become legal at midnight.

'Now tell me exactly what happened at Greenfields,' Conran said to him.

Paul recounted the story. They were half-way along Kensington High Street, weaving in and out of the traffic, by the time he had finished. The security man made no comment. All he did was give Paul a long, hard look.

'Did Stapleton and Ferris know all along what Larke was at?' Paul asked after a moment.

'I don't think so.' Conran seemed preoccupied, looking out over the driver's shoulder as they approached Knightsbridge. 'Not till they saw your story in the paper.

They must have questioned Larke, and either he or Drummond told them the truth. Since the Regiment of God was about to be enriched by five million pounds, they had no choice but to try to silence you.'

Paul sat thinking. 'There's no possibility that the Confederation for International Studies had condoned Larke's experiment?'

'That's an outrageous suggestion,' Conran replied angrily. 'You're fantasising, Mr Marriott. Take it from me, Larke and Drummond acted entirely on their own.'

Paul said no more. He only wondered how Conran had been so well informed about Larke's activities and why he had seemed so unenthusiastic about ordering the arrest of Stapleton and Ferris.

A few minutes later they turned into Wilton Place, then came to Belgrave Square.

'Drive right around,' Conran said. 'It's on the other side.'

There was no traffic, not a soul to be seen, as they approached General Stapleton's house. 'Park in on the left there,' Conran said.

The car slid to a stop by the garden railings.

'Now put your headlights on.'

The lights came on. Nicola stirred and put her arm through Paul's. No one spoke. There was only the click and sweep of the screenwipers, the rain hammering on the car roof. Conran was sitting forward again looking intently out through the window.

After a long time a Mini appeared, going fairly fast and making for the north side of the square. As it went by, its headlamps flashed briefly.

'Follow it,' Conran ordered.

They kept twenty or thirty yards behind the little car as it drove along Wilton Place. At Motcomb Street it turned left, then swung into the narrow length of Kinnerton Street. Still going fast, it continued ɔr about a hundred yards, sweeping past the rain-drencl d facades of mews cottages, the glow of the Knightsbridge street-lamps visible above the rooftops beyond. Then the Mini braked sharply, drove into an empty garage yard and stopped.

The security car pulled in on the other side of the yard and Conran leaned across Paul and Nicola to lower the window. A woman had got out of the Mini and was coming towards them; she was wearing a leather coat, a scarf tied under her chin. As she approached, Paul recognised her. It was Molly, the woman who had called off the thugs outside Chepstow House the night before.

She put her head down to the window and spoke quickly to Conran. 'I could only give Periscope Three a flash, sir. There were two of O'Connor's boys in a van parked at the corner of Chapel Street . . .'

'What is it?' Conran asked.

'A bomb in General Stapleton's car. Probably a time fuse, I don't know. I couldn't budge with the bloody van there . . .'

'All right.' Conran turned quickly to the driver. 'The M4,' he said.

The car backed up and they headed for Knightsbridge again.

'Call Periscope Central,' Conran told the radio operator. 'Urgent and copy Periscope Three and Information Room. Put them in the picture.'

As they joined the Knightsbridge traffic, the operator spoke through his microphone. 'Periscope One to Periscope Central. Over.'

'Periscope Central. Yes, Periscope One? Over.'

'Origin Periscope One twenty-o-four. Urgent and copy Periscope Three and Information Room. Rolls Bentley ARJ 607D heading M4 is carrying lollipop, flavour unknown. Lollipop, flavour unknown. Over.'

'Periscope Central to Periscope One. Understood. Over.'

They crawled along Knightsbridge, the traffic almost solid, the rain deluging down.

'How will they handle this, sir?' the man in the far

corner of the seat asked quietly.

'Try to isolate the car. Get it in the open. Close a section of the motorway.' Conran seemed to be talking half to himself. 'But they'll have to work fast. It's almost certainly a time device. There was no opportunity to wire the car. . . . See if you can get Periscope Three.' he said to the radio operator.

'Periscope One to Periscope Three. Over . . . Periscope One to Periscope Three. Over . . .' The man went on repeating the call. But there was no answer. 'I expect they're talking to Information Room,' he said to Conran.

Conran continued to sit forward, clasping and unclasping his hands in front of him. They had got no further than Harrods, the traffic at a standstill now. Nicola kept her arm through Paul's, sitting very still, staring at the lighted windows of the shops. They edged on a few more yards then stopped again. Several minutes passed.

The radio crackled suddenly. 'Periscope Three to Periscope One. Over.'

The operator jabbed a switch. 'Periscope Three. Yes?'

'Copied your origin twenty-o-four. We are near Chiswick flyover. Lollipop car fifty yards ahead. Traffic blocked and stationary. Awaiting MP cars. Over.'

The rain, Paul thought. The rain and the weekend. It could take Larke another twenty minutes to reach the motorway. He wondered if O'Connor's boys had thought of that. Probably they hadn't cared. Gerald McDermot's car had been completely demolished in the Hampstead explosion, he recalled. He doubted if there would be less than twenty pounds of gelignite in the back of the Bentley. 'What about Bomb Disposal?' he said to Conran.

'They've got to get there,' Conran said viciously. 'And they can't defuse the bomb in the middle of a traffic jam. If it goes up on the flyover, we'll have a bloody disaster on our hands.'

Paul looked past Nicola out of the window. It wasn't difficult to picture the scene: lines of wrecked and burning cars, exploding petrol tanks, the flyover blocked and inaccessible to ambulances and fire engines.

Conran turned his head briefly, his face white and drawn-looking in the lamplight. 'All this because you had to go blabbing to your communist friends. Whose side are you supposed to be on, I'd like to know?'

Paul didn't answer. It seemed hardly the moment to make a policy statement. In any case he didn't think Conran would appreciate it. He was aware of Nicola watching him from the corner of the seat. He was on the side of people like Rosamond Clay and Jack Tendler, he thought; of John Aubrey and all the youngsters who were being battened on by the fast-buck heroin-pushers; of exploited illegal immigrants and the victims of bent policemen; of simple, competent family-loving men like Arthur Frewin. Unlike God, he was on the side of the small battalions. He said, 'Never mind whose side I'm on. What about people like Stapleton and Ferris, so anxious to preserve Britain, democracy, their privileges or whatever — shouldn't they be a little more careful in their choice of friends?'

Conran said nothing, staring over the driver's shoulder. They had almost reached the end of Brompton Road. After a moment he turned to the radio operator. 'Try to get a situation report,' he ordered.

'Periscope One to Periscope Central. Over.'

'Periscope Central. Over.'

'Sit rep, please. Over.'

'Central to Periscope One. Hammersmith and Chiswick MP cars are diverting traffic from both flyovers. Congestion bad to severe. Lollipop car will be flagged on to motorway and followed by MP patrols. Intercept by Disposal Squad anticipated once clear of buildings. Repeat, congestion bad to severe. Central over.'

The going improved a little as they reached Cromwell Road. Then they ran into another snarl-up just short of the Air Terminal.

191

'We've got to get out of this damned traffic,' Conran said suddenly. 'Operator–call Information Room, see if they can provide an escort.'

The operator was through to Scotland Yard in a matter of seconds. 'Periscope One to Information Room. Our origin twenty-o-five. We are near Cromwell Road Air Terminal, grey Rover 3500 KSB 914R. Can you provide escort? Over.'

'Information Room to Periscope One. Your origin twenty-o-five. Stand by. MP over.'

It was a full five minutes before they came back. 'Periscope One. Your origin twenty-o-five. MP cars escorting Disposal Squad will pick you up Cromwell Road. Flash headlamps to identify. MP over.'

A moment later they heard the sirens and the driver started flashing his lights. A police car went by, closely followed by a red-painted Land-Rover of Bomb Disposal. A second squad car stopped behind them and Conran's driver pulled out.

Though the traffic was heavy going out of town, there wasn't all that much coming in. With the police car ahead clearing the way, they made slow but steady progress at first. There were some hold-ups between West Kensington and Baron's Court while the convoy stood with beacons flashing and sirens wailing until the on-coming cars opened a path for them. The radio operator was keeping his set tuned in to Information Room, the curiously detached voices of the controllers and squad car men crackling through the speaker. A dialogue of life and death. The lollipop car was now only twenty yards from the diversion point on the Chiswick flyover. It had been on the road for forty minutes.

As they approached Hammersmith, the road cleared suddenly and they picked up speed. The cars on the inside lane were being diverted at the Hammersmith flyover, those on the outside lane at Chiswick. They crossed the first flyover unhindered and soon saw two more police cars in front of them.

Conran hadn't moved since they had picked up the escort. He was sitting right forward with his hands on the front seat, looking fixedly through the rain-glitter of the windscreen. It was almost as if he could hear the bomb ticking hurriedly away in the back of the Bentley.

They came to the Chiswick flyover and sped past a crawling line of cars. A road beacon had been set up by the turn-off at the far end, a squad car parked beyond it. Two policemen were directing the traffic on to the slip road while a third stood watching a little way up the line. Craning his neck over the radio operator's shoulder, Paul saw the third policeman step forward suddenly and hold up his hand. There was a car moving away just in front of him; it was approaching the slip road when the other two men stepped back and flagged it on towards the motorway. He recognised the big, solid shape of a Rolls Bentley.

'Lollipop car clear. Following. MP over.'

They were close behind the red Land-Rover as it swung past the beacon and headed after the other squad cars. The lead car was slackening speed, keeping nearly a hundred yards behind the Bentley.

'Information Room to Disposal Squad. Stand by to intercept. MP over.'

The controllers were taking a calculated risk. For the next two miles or so the road passed through a heavily built-up area. Only after that would the Bentley reach the open countryside. A few extra minutes, a few more turns of the timing mechanism wired to the detonator of the bomb.

Larke must have realised that something was wrong. The main stream of traffic hadn't followed him off the flyover. Though there were no sirens now, he had evidently seen the beacons on the police cars behind him. As if to test the situation, he put on speed.

The lead car maintained its distance. They were doing

nearly seventy, heading for the Hogarth roundabout that would take them through Brentford to the beginning of the main motorway.

Nicola lurched against Paul as, tyres squealing, they negotiated the roundabout. Conran was holding on to the front seat, still gazing intently through the twin half-moons made by the wiper blades. They sped on. The blue-flashing beacon on the roof of the Land-Rover threw a pulsating light into the car, quick as a frightened heart-beat.

A household alarm clock taped with two torch batteries to twenty pounds of gelignite; wires leading from the batteries to a brass detonator buried in the explosive; a small piece of solder on the face of the clock. When the minute hand touched the solder, the circuit would be closed and the detonator would fire. It was probably something as simple as that. A bomb big enough to blow out the front of an average-sized suburban villa. Put together in the back room of some cheap lodging house by men nourished on an ancient and now meaningless tribal hatred. As Larke gunned the big car towards the motor-way, millimetre by millimetre the minute hand was creeping towards the bright blob of metal.

'Come on!' Conran said fiercely under his breath. 'Now! Come on!'

The Bentley, a hundred and fifty yards in front of them, had reached the start of the three-lane carriageway. On either side there were trees now, fields, a golf course.

'Information Room to Disposal Squad. Intercept. Over.'

The Land-Rover pulled out. Siren whooping, it began to overtake the squad cars. Conran put his hand up to wipe his face. At that very moment the Bentley exploded. A lurid, blinding flash and the car seemed to buck, its rear wheels lifting off the ground for an instant. Slewing wildly round, it careered across the road, hit the crash barrier and turned over in a sheet of orange flame.

194

As they drew nearer there was little to be seen but fire and smoke, the underside of the chassis bared grotesquely to the rain-filled sky. They stopped and Paul climbed from the car with Nicola. Conran pushed past them and hurried up the road to where some policemen were standing, dark shapes against the brilliant, dancing flames.

Paul went a little way after Conran and paused, looking at the wreckage. He thought of Diana Beresford, the woman whose bed he had shared only a few nights before; of Antonia Unwin whom he had never seen, the last of the night's innocent victims. For the general and his soldier friends, a truly Siegfriedian end. Perhaps Nietzsche would have approved.

He came back to Nicola and put an arm round her shoulder. They waited. More cars arrived, a fire engine; beacons were set up in the middle of the carriageway. The scene was a chaos of glaring, pulsing light patterns and huge, weirdly moving shadows, black drifting smoke and the smell of burning rubber.

Conran rejoined them ten minutes later. His collar turned up against the rain, he stopped beside Paul. 'Something to put in your newspaper, Mr Marriott,' he said sourly.

'All right. Now throw the D notices at me.'

Conran spoke quickly and mechanically, looking at the ground in front of him. 'Nothing about brainwashing with the use of drugs. No mention of hallucinogens or psycho-technology. Larke's methods must not be specified. You can make something up, I don't care. No word about the Confederation for International Studies and their rela-tionship with the security services. I think that's all.'

A car had drawn up near by and a policewoman was coming towards them. 'The car to take you home, Miss Clay,' Conran said and walked off.

Paul went to the car. As the policewoman climbed into the back seat, Nicola turned suddenly and impulsively and put her arms around him.

He held her for a moment, her slender body pressed against his own. 'You were great,' he said. 'You were a marvel, you really were.'

She looked up at him, her eyes filled with tears, her face pathetically child-like and exhausted-looking in the confused light. 'Paul . . .'

He bent forward and kissed her cheek. 'We'll keep in touch, love,' he said.

He helped her in beside the policewoman and slammed the door. As the car drove away, he could see her watching him through the rear window.

He had nearly an hour left of Chris's cocktail, he thought as he stepped out of a squad car and climbed the stairway to his flat. Letting himself in, he switched on the hall and passage lights and went to the living room.

In a moment he would call the paper and dictate his story. He knew exactly what he was going to say; every word, every paragraph was clear in his mind. They would have an exclusive on the M4 bombing. It gave him some satisfaction to think that Plummer, his mouth full of chocolate biscuits, was going to have to change the front page.

Crossing, he turned on the radio. In a couple of minutes the news would be on. He was interested to learn if the BBC had picked anything up and, if so, what the official line had been. He waited. After a few seconds the sound of pop music came loud from the set.

> Yes! Yes! I want someone to love!
> Somone to cry with,
> Live till I die with,
> Someone to love.

Standing in the middle of the half-lit room, he listened to the song.

Someone to sing with,
Have me a fling with,
Someone to love.
Someone to walk with,
Someone to talk with,
Someone to love.
Yes! Yes! I want someone to love!

As the music began to fade, he heard a noise coming from somewhere at the back of the flat. The rush and thump of the storm wind.

He left the living room and went along the two passageways to the kitchen.

Entering the scullery, he closed the window and turned round. The air about him was freezing cold. For a few seconds he stood looking across the dim, confined space.

'Hello, Fred me old cock,' he said quietly. 'How's things?'